Out of Season

OUT OF SEASON

Stories

Kirk Wilson

ELIXIR PRESS
Denver, Colorado

OUT OF SEASON. Copyright © 2023 by Kirk Wilson.
First published by Elixir Press, Denver, Colorado.

Designed by Steven Seighman
Front cover art by Kyle McBride

ISBN: 978-1-932-41880-4

Library of Congress Cataloging-in-Publication Data
Names: Wilson, Kirk, 1946- author.
Title: Out of season : stories / Kirk Wilson.
Description: First edition. | Denver, Colorado : Elixir Press, 2022. |
Summary: "Winner of the Elixir Press Fiction Award short stories"--
Provided by publisher.
Identifiers: LCCN 2022027044 | ISBN 9781932418804 (paperback)
Subjects: LCGFT: Short stories.
Classification: LCC PS3573.I4574 O98 2022 | DDC 813/.54--dc23/eng/20220617
LC record available at https://lccn.loc.gov/2022027044

First Edition: 2023

10   9   8   7   6   5   4   3   2   1

For Donna and our children and theirs

"I did believe in vain gestures. I did believe in fate."
—ROBERTO BOLAÑO, in *Antwerp*

"Strange violin, are you following me?"
—RAINER MARIA RILKE, in "The Neighbor"

Contents

Out of Season

Tapioca

The botanist made a lot of money breeding soybeans that would grow in dust.

He didn't care much for the money and had no interest in knowing how much of it he had.

He lived in a cheap motel and wore clothes from second-hand stores.

His advancement in soybean horticulture came through a combination of seed science and shamanism.

He was self-taught in both fields.

He did not own a car.

He took his meals in a nearby cafeteria known for its mediocre food.

He did the same things every day in the same order so that he did not have to think about those things and could reserve thought time for things that interested him.

He was not against variety.

In certain frames of mind he had the battered cod with tartar sauce instead of the roast beef with gravy the black eyed peas instead of the green beans and the mac and cheese instead of the mashed potatoes.

He always had the tapioca pudding.

One day at lunch he learned the cafeteria was closing.

Cafeterias were going out of style.

The lease was up and the owner of the cafeteria could no longer afford the payments.

There were rumors of developments in the area and the property owner wanted to cash in.

The botanist bought the cafeteria and the land it stood on.

He had to outbid many interested parties and pay a ridiculous price.

He didn't care.

It wasn't about money.

It was about a place to eat.

He kept the entire staff in place and gave everyone a raise.

He told the manager he didn't want to change a thing.

One day a representative of a developer approached him as he carried his tray from the service line to his accustomed table.

The developer planned to build a major residential and retail environment that would swallow everything in sight and the cafeteria occupied a tiny fraction near the center of its intended footprint.

The representative powered up her tablet and explained how transformative the development will be.

This entire section of the city will be made anew.

Eyesores will be eliminated undesirables cast out jobs created lives fulfilled property values will explode economies will boom.

She showed the botanist pictures of glistening jewelry counters au courant restaurants splendid homes beneath benevolent sunsets skywalks skytrams palatial malls children on amusement rides with parents drunk on happiness parks soccer fields ice rinks.

Imagine all that here around us.

How awesome how truly unbelievably awesome it will be.

The representative was authorized to present an offer on the spot that would bring the botanist a far far more than handsome profit on his investment in the property.

She touched the screen to reveal a page covered with a supersize dollar sign and a long line of tall numbers divided by commas.

Wasn't that exciting.

The botanist said thanks for coming by but the cafeteria was not for sale and chewed another mouthful of his mac and cheese.

During the presentation he had realized a new way to encourage a seed to ignore conditions it might have otherwise abhorred and imagine a life for itself on its own terms.

The representative noticed that the botanist ate each item on his tray separately and did not partake of another item until he was finished with the first.

The developer sent a series of escalating offers and the botanist turned them all down.

The developer couldn't believe it.

Soon all the land necessary for the development was in hand except the tiny portion that held the cafeteria.

The developer's machines were busy knocking things down and excavating holes across the landscape.

It was good old-fashioned plundering with better tools.

There were only a handful of regular patrons left anyway but even these could not come near the cafeteria because all the streets were blocked off and to walk among the machines was to take your life in your hands.

In an epiphany the developer realized the problem.

The botanist must not know who he was dealing with.

He told his assistant to send the botanist links to the many pages of online information about himself his accomplishments and his company.

But the botanist did not own a smart phone or computer and had no use for the internet.

The developer sent the assistant to the cafeteria with a glossy brochure that told his life story in heroic prose with accompanying photographs of his developments and himself at various life stages.

The assistant had to pick her way around the giant machines which resembled lumbering and dutiful exoskeletal creatures with excellent work ethics.

The botanist was now the only customer in his cafeteria.

The assistant joined him at his table.

The noise of the machines at work outside bombarded the walls in a way that made it hard to carry on a conversation.

The botanist glanced at the brochure.

He wasn't out to judge but he did have opinions.

In his opinion the brochure was waste of trees puffery about a mindless transient busy trashing a small but previously lovely planet orbiting an unremarkable star in deep space.

Ants who spit formic acid to coincidentally or perhaps in an intentionally helpful way improve the pH of soil and meet the needs of orchids were more interesting.

Photosynthesis was much much more interesting.

The botanist offered the assistant a bowl of tapioca pudding which she declined.

The developer increased his offers by twenty percent each time the botanist said no.

He went up fifty percent to no avail.

He threw in a small ownership stake in the development.

He thought the botanist was playing him.

The assistant said she was happy to keep making the increasingly difficult trips to the cafeteria but she really really thought the botanist would never sell no matter what.

The developer fired the assistant.

He sent new offers to the motel via Certified Mail.

The botanist refused to sign for the envelopes.

The developer drove his Maserati to the motel himself with an offer of obscene proportions in his pocket.

The botanist looked out from behind a curtain but would not come to the door.

The developer was so aggravated he lost control of the car in an intersection and T-boned a city bus.

He had never faced such an impediment.

It was crazy.

So was he.

He suffered from extreme mood swings and didn't like the way his meds made him feel.

It was already hard enough to get things done.

The whole world had turned against him.

It was pissed.

Birds and other animals were dropping dead all over.

But that had no effect on the development business.

It just weakened the argument for trees.

People were dropping dead too.

But not people who mattered.

Other things did matter.

Things that weighed on his business like a worldwide saturated towel.

Property-eating tornadoes twirled where they never had before.

Oceans which had previously become angry only with the trespasses of individual mariners or occasional invading armadas now swelled with anger against everything especially property in cities anywhere near a coast.

Deadly germs outsmarted every medicine.

A city might have been buried under ash before but now whole countries burned or froze or burned *and* froze.

Refugees swarmed away from wars starvation burning freezing and disrupted business on all sides.

The developer didn't care.

He was pissed too.

He was super big and super rich and he planned to own a whole lot more of everything before he died.

No cafeteria was going to stop him.

The moment he got back in his office after the wreck he grabbed a burner phone and called the security guy he paid to protect himself and things he owned and intimidate people who got in his way.

The security guy was a former Israeli intelligence officer who had converted to Holy Ghost Prosperity Nondenominationalism.

He had come to America to rewrite his destiny.

It was working pretty well.

He had acquired a new five bedroom house with four bedrooms that were never used a new beautiful young wife who spent money in impressive ways and his own new office building with the name of his company on top.

The developer was his biggest client.

The developer told him what he wanted.

The security guy said he was talking about an extremely dangerous sensitive and tricky operation that would cost a lot of money.

The developer didn't care.

He put an extremely lucrative bounty on the table.

The security guy hired two former Navy Seals he knew through church to carry out a contract hit on the botanist.

The Seals were bored in their civilian lives.

The bounty exceeded not only the value of the cafeteria real estate but all of the grossly inflated offers the developer had made.

Plus a bonus at the developer's discretion for a job well done.

The Seals could retire in luxury anywhere they chose.

They spent a week tracking their target's movements.

In their spare time they looked online at Lamborghinis and speedboats.

The target's activities hardly varied from one day to the next.

The Seals thoroughly cased the motel the cafeteria and other locations the target favored and created a chronological spreadsheet of his daily habits.

They reviewed potential strategies with the security guy.

The Seals preferred a straightforward assassination.

A quick hit using silenced pistols or a sniper rifle fired from a nearby parking garage.

Or a slit throat.

Or garroting with piano wire.

The former intelligence agent nixed these unimaginative suggestions.

He preferred a nuanced approach that brought with it the virtue of being undetectable and thus unprovable.

He revealed that he had in his possession an ultrafine powder containing a super deadly nerve agent he had acquired from a Russian contact.

He kept the powder in a perfume bottle in his office safe.

His plan involved treating the tapioca pudding the target carried on his plastic tray twice each day at the cafeteria with the tiny required amount of the tasteless and odorless nerve agent.

One Seal would distract the target while the other dusted the tapioca.

The Seals thought the plan was borderline effeminate but said nothing due to the chain of command and the size of the bounty.

The security guy was proud of the plan.

He thought it was excellent.

The developer thought so too.

In a clandestine meeting in a parking lot the day before the developer had demanded to know exactly what the plan was.

The security guy told him he didn't need to know.

Really really shouldn't know.

It wasn't smart.

The developer didn't care.

He was paying a lot of money and wanted to know what he was buying.

When he found out he was so happy he laughed until he cried.

He loved loved loved that the hit would happen in the cafeteria during the first bite of the botanist's dessert.

He was riding right on the crest of a big happy manic episode.

He leaned one hand on a nearby car and wiped tears from his cheeks with the back of his other hand.

He gave the security guy a hard collegial slap on the shoulder.

The slap really stung but the security guy was tough and didn't show it.

The slapping hand was overlarge.

The developer had been a football hero in college and the NFL.

He had been known as The Claw for his ability to trap opposing quarterbacks in the talons of his hands and crush them beneath his hypermuscled weight.

His doctor thought his mood swing issues were amplified by brain damage suffered in hundreds of helmet to helmet encounters.

The doctor said nothing because he was himself a fan and the developer was a true football hero.

Nostalgia for the developer's glorious achievements on the field gave him a potent advantage in business.

It also served as a bond between himself and the security guy.

In the first waves of immigrant enthusiasm for his adopted country the security guy had become gravely addicted to American football.

To him the developer was a genuine celebrity.

Still basking in the glow of the celebrity's giddy delight about his plan he took the perfume bottle from the safe to show the Seals.

The Dallas Cowboys were playing the Kansas City Chiefs on the screen mounted on his office wall.

A game of cowboys and Indians portrayed by brutal gladiators in a coliseum.

The attraction was irresistible.

When the Seals left the meeting the security guy lost himself in the game because it had gone into overtime and left the perfume bottle sitting out on his credenza.

He had never made a mistake of this magnitude in his entire career.

Such was the hold football had over him.

He went home to dinner with his wife and her visiting sister.

The even younger and more beautiful sister had flown half-way 'round the world.

It was her first time in America.

The next day while he was calling on a client his assistant treated the sister to a tour of the new office building.

Left on her own for a moment in the security guy's office she helped herself to a lethal sniff from the bottle.

The Yorkie terrier she carried in her arms also perished.

The security guy had to bring in a special team in hazmat gear to clean the office.

The team incinerated the perfume bottle and its contents.

The security guy had a very delicate conversation with his wife which did not go as well as he had hoped.

He denied all knowledge but the marriage wasn't perfect anyway and the wife divorced him and returned to her family.

He couldn't afford to fight over the assets because the wife knew too much.

His net worth took a massive hit.

He abandoned the tapioca strategy.

The cause of the sister in law's death was never determined.

The dog's simultaneous death was thought to be a strange coincidence.

As a child the botanist spent all the time he was allowed in the outdoors.

Mornings took hold of him and drew him to the ground.

He spent days on his hands and knees discovering.

Walking upright he missed too much.

Acorns were a special fascination.

His mother came across small cities of them hidden under clothing in his dresser drawers.

An acorn made an oak tree.

The scale and precision of this process held the botanist's imagination as a nest holds an egg.

He understood the process but did not know its cause.

The cause clearly did not begin with the seed and did not end with the tree.

He thought he saw the process reflected in the sky above especially the thing it did at night when the painted curtain vanished and the endless speckled whole fell open.

That was a way of looking at it.

But not a way of touching it.

The sky pulled him but the ground pulled him harder.

On the ground he felt the process moving.

Even if he didn't know its cause and was left wanting to know so much it hurt him.

He was a small nearsighted boy who became a small nearsighted man.

The dust foretold his future.

The developer was severely displeased to learn that the plan for the hit had been abandoned.

He took it as further evidence that the world had turned against him.

His mood had swung into depression.

A pit deeper and darker than the deepest and darkest.

He hated everything and everyone most especially himself.

He expressed his hatred by punching holes through walls and lashing out at anyone in reach.

Many people would have been in reach if they were not avoiding him.

One who could not avoid him was the security guy.

Who was at that point in the early days of his extremely expensive divorce.

The developer called and threatened to pull the contract unless the security guy made the botanist dead within three days.

And to personally jump on a bulldozer and knock down the security guy's house.

This threat happened to be empty because the security guy was losing the house in the divorce and now stayed in a lonely apartment where he questioned all his life decisions to date.

The rewrite of his destiny had hit a very bad patch.

The bank was about to foreclose on the office building.

Before he punched off the developer tossed in a threat to sue for nonperformance.

The security guy knew the developer was famous for suing people.

He did not pay his suppliers and when they sued for payment he countersued and harassed them until he drove them out of business.

The security guy also knew that nobody sued for nonperformance of a hit.

But he didn't say so.

He really needed the money at this point.

He assured the developer there was nothing to worry about.

It was all taken care of.

He didn't need to know the details.

It really really was best if he didn't.

The security guy held his breath waiting for the developer to demand the details anyway.

He didn't know how he would respond.

He had been distracted by the turmoil in his own life and hadn't done a thing about the hit.

Luckily the developer was too depressed to talk anymore.

He threw down the phone and sat for a long time staring at his trophies.

Meanwhile the Seals were getting antsy.

They figured the sister in law's death could very well lead to the whole deal unraveling and the two of them landing in prison.

They looked into ways to leave the country for someplace with no extradition agreements.

They only stayed because they couldn't bear to give up the bounty.

The security guy called them into a meeting.

He told them they were back at square one and he had too much shit to deal with and they were on their own.

He didn't want to know how they did it he just wanted it done.

He said they had three days max.

And if they blew it he had ways to get to them wherever they were even in a cell and make sure they didn't talk.

He suggested that they all join hands and pray.

Which they did.

They knew the game had gone into overtime.

And time was running out.

It was racing past them like a Lambo or a speedboat.

For the botanist time had the texture of a loose familiar garment.

It was never in a hurry.

It was uncluttered.

So was space.

The motel room was spare.

The only items the botanist owned were his clothes his toiletries his notebooks and some pens.

Even these he did not think of as belonging to him.

There was a bed and an unassuming dresser and a desk with a straight-back chair.

He had moved out the TV and the armchair.

There were three books borrowed each week from the university library and returned for three more and kept in a neat stack on the desk. Outside along the wall there were several rows of seedlings in miniature greenhouses the botanist constructed himself.

As a relatively small person the botanist was drawn to relatively small things.

Of course there was always the question of relative to what.

Relative to the cosmos all things are small although the cosmos has a place in the story of all smaller things and thus is relative always to itself.

The seedlings didn't care that they were in the parking lot of a cheap motel.

They thought they owned the place and made their own decisions.

Each of their lives was an infinitely variable story.

The weather was changing.

Lately it had become undependable but today it changed in a dependable way with one season announcing its displacement of another.

Leaves skipped across the motel parking lot.

The botanist was struck even then by the freshness of things.

He picked up a leaf and read it sentence by sentence without hurrying.

The developer could not bear to let things sit.

Places needed him to change them.

Things had to be torn up.

He had to stay busy.

No one asked him why he was this way.

If they had he might have said it was his brother.

He told himself so when he had too much to drink.

He had an older brother he worshipped who also played football.

Who died in a car smashup with his girlfriend under his armpit when he was in high school.

So the developer lived to do all his brother never could.

Played the hell out of football in college.

Played like the devil himself in the NFL.

Beat the development business like a drum.

All to impress the brother because he is older though dead.

All to give the brother something to live up to because he is younger forever and can never grow older.

The absent everpresent strangeness of an older younger brother who was the reason for everything reached beyond the developer's understanding.

When he thought of it he wept.

Alcohol and mood swings were factors.

The way he felt about the enigma of his brother was more or less the way the botanist felt about the movement of the endless process he observed.

Something you carried with you that carried you with it.

Something you could feel but never comprehend.

Something so elusive yet so close you had it and missed it all at once so much you never stopped aching.

In this way the developer and the botanist were alike.

The Seals could not sit still.

Their bodies jumped with anxiety.

The feeling was unprecedented.

They did not know what to call it.

After all this thing they had to do was nothing.

They had been under fire.

They had slaughtered the enemy and sometimes the innocent.

The innocents were collateral damage.

They had carried the bodies of their buddies from the field.

They had done this for America.

They were soldiers.

They had seen far worse.

But it was as if they had done nothing and remembered nothing and spent their waking and their sleeping hours struggling to forget nothing.

They watched the botanist through their binoculars bending over his greenhouses like a little god.

They felt little too like boys who were excited but afraid.

Like dark insignificant points too small to be recognized by a spy satellite from space.

They didn't talk about it but they carried buried inside them the thought that though they had killed for America they had never killed for money.

This was all about the money.

It was best to keep the money foremost in their thoughts.

But the other thought the one buried inside them made them afraid of themselves and they hated that.

They hated the botanist for making them feel that way.

People seemed to think this was a human world.

In the botanist's opinion it was a life world.

He knew what seeds did after the plant of which they were a member as continuous as a hand or a tongue withered and disintegrated.

The thing about life is it keeps trying.

Until eventually something catches on and drags itself over the horizon.

You can knock it back but you can't stop it.

You could spray all the insecticide you liked on bugs and though the bugs you sprayed might die their friends and relations only came back stronger in greater numbers.

And germs would do the same no matter what kind of antibiotic you fed them.

The botanist observed the process of the life world and noted its connective texture but did not know its cause.

The human world thought was people's great mistake.

It drove them to be disconnected.

To pave and air-condition and mold things in their own images.

Deep inside they realized the mistake but were unable to do anything about it.

They knew the place they lived did not belong to them.

They could keep remodeling it until it was unlivable and life wouldn't care.

It would just go on without them.

The Seals decided to keep things simple.

When night fell they walked up to the door and knocked.

The botanist was seated at the desk reading and taking notes in his journal.

For company he had several shallow bowls of seeds beside him.

The greenhouse seedlings were asleep.

So were the exoskeletal machines outside the cafeteria.

The developer was in his office with the talons of The Claw gripped around a championship commemorative football.

There were tears in his eyes.

The security guy was watching Jeopardy in his apartment.

There was no game on.

The falling night took hold of the botanist and drew him to the ground.

He could feel the process moving.

He understood its movement but did not know its cause.

The Seals didn't speak to one another as they left.

One of them tried to think about the Lambo the other the speedboat.

Banquo's Ghost

Tejada writes:

Roger is exhausted. He reclines on a deck chair above his swimming pool. Intended as a celebration, the election-watching party turned into a debacle, and went on too long. Guests—mostly Natalie's colleagues—lingered with gut-punched expressions, drinking unwisely. The ghosts of their bewilderment now inhabit crumbed plates and stemmed glasses with half-moons of wine, abandoned on the rented bar tables that surround Roger's chair.

There, Tejada thinks, it's started. He is besieged by this story, has held it at bay long enough. Facing any story to the end is difficult, but in this one he must play the perpetrator who betrays and badly wounds his friend and champion, the first critic north of Mexico to recognize his work. Revenge is a lifeless reason for a story, like building a gun made of words. But now he knows how the thing begins and has to find out how it ends.

I love Natalie because she is of my soul, Tejada says. *Not to mention helpful for my meager sales. Roger I admit because she loves him, but do not welcome or forgive.*

Tejada, whose grandmother spoke Nahuat, is not impressed that Roger speaks the better Spanish of the two. Natalie has been married to Roger for almost thirty years. She is twenty years behind him on the path to invisibility. Both are famous in small ways. Natalie is the world's authority on the Salvadoran fabulist Tejada, a person of one name. Roger is a VIP emeritus of the American elite that, until tonight, held off its enemies without and within, and deflected the worst impulses of the populace. He once upon a time ran the government's clandestine services in the Caribbean and Latin America—and yes, that includes *clandestine services* inside Tejada's country. Only Natalie has been previously married. They have no children.

A neighbor's backyard security light winks on the surface of the water. A bird calls, or an insect, *chi whee chi.* The limbs of oaks and elms reach out to form a canopy. In warmer weather, Roger likes to swim on his back looking up at the underside of the leaves. Often he imagines floating off from there.

When he does succeed in floating off, Tejada thinks that Roger thinks, Natalie will miss him, but she lives more or less exclusively between her ears, and the idea of him can stick around to keep her company. And of course she will always have Tejada, who, Roger suspects, is more important to her anyway. Tejada, when he floats, will no doubt savor the idea of being an idea. An afterlife devoutly to be wished.

Roger folds his hands together like birds that might escape. He surveys the rock wall that runs around the backside of the pool. Below it a ravine falls sharply to a creek bed, a steep but not impossible climb. The shouts of a drunken argument reach him, from deep in the ravine. A band of homeless people often camp there in a patch of woods. When the limbs are bare, as they soon will be, he can look over the top of his wall and make out the detritus of their lives through the branches of the trees: muddy blankets, beer cans, wine bottles, candy wrappers, a mattress made of leaves. Roger has no quarrel with the homeless. He and Natalie make sandwiches for them weekly, at their church. He watches them not because he considers them a threat, but because they stand as a factor in his equations, an indicator of the

weather. So long as the trees stay rooted in their places and the camp-
ers stay among them, he can abide. He has known dangerous people.
These are not them.

The voices turn to water, and he drifts but does not float. His
thoughts lose their linkages and his breathing goes shallow. Before
long he is opening the door to the room of the neglected animals.
Tejada is familiar with Roger's worst dream, and does not want
to witness it again. Yet here it comes. A keeper's room most often
underground, full of starving dogs, parrots stiff as mummies on
the floors of cages, a paralytic mountain lion wrapped in a valley
of bones. The smell of waste is so thick the dreamer must push
through it with his hands, through air that is a deep and viscous
blue. Roger is the abject keeper. The suffering he is compelled to
witness is his responsibility.

Tejada cannot stay long in this story. He walks away from it. De-
compresses in his modest orchard with its colliding smells of ripe fruit
and diesel exhaust. Opens the book he has left on a bench and reads
the Jiménez poem called *"Oceans."*

> *I have a feeling that my boat*
> *has struck, down there in the depths,*
> *against a great thing.*
> > *And nothing*
> *happens! Nothing...Silence...Waves...*
>
> *—Nothing happens? Or has everything happened,*
> *And are we standing now, quietly, in the new life?*

Finally he returns, like an obstinate child to his lessons, to the deck
above the pool, where Roger waits in the dark of his dream, agitated
and alone. *I owe you nothing*, Tejada tells him.

But he writes:

Here is something to know about Roger. He takes a disagreeable pleasure in the fact that he has seen this night on the horizon, has traced its currents and charted its approach the way a meteorologist does a weather system. The agency that was his lifework will now be run by traitorous thugs, and empty-chested thieves will take the benches of the courts. The ideologues of Roger's day were dangerous enough. These are the locusts of doom. He sees it, he has seen it, but it can't be happening. The American experiment, with all its aspirations, is too young to sputter toward a final precipice.

Tejada thinks: *The story is impossible. They will say the voice is not mine.* But he writes:

Here is another thing to know about Roger. Upstairs in this house, beside his bed, he keeps a nun three inches tall who glows in the dark. She stands beneath a bedside lamp, facing him, her hands joined in prayer. When he switches off the light she turns glow-stick green and her form softens as if she is radiating care into the room. For a while she is the only thing he sees.

Does the intercession of the little nun redeem him? Tejada wonders. It's possible, but too early to know. One thing is certain: Tejada will be attacked for this story, not because people do not understand it, but because they understand it too well.

Will Natalie defend him, as she always has? It will be a test for her, of how objective and professional she can be. The attacks may cost her more than they cost him. Too bad her lingo, reserved as it is for the cosseted elect who form her audience, will fly over heads and land somewhere in the clouds. He is hopeful as he imagines her response.

Yes, Tejada has intruded here. Violated confidences and used, some would say cruelly misused, those who have long supported his work. But the story was there to be written, and the world has given him cruel stories to write. Think of his melancholy colonels, weirdly compelling perpetrators of massacre and assassination. Like those characters, the melancholy perpetrator here has harrowed many and brought chaos down upon Tejada's people. *But this new protagonist compares to those earlier ones in only epidermal ways. He and his wife are not only the first North Americans in the stories. They are new creatures in Tejada's world, Daedalian mutants who may be seen to generate an abjection in the post-structural sense.* Take that! Tejada thinks. *An abjection! I'll have to look it up to be sure I know what it means.*

Natalie keeps her first marriage in a wicker box, a world of thirty-seven antique letters ordered by their postmark dates. They arrived every few days, for six months and one week, with the same stick figure cartoon of the two of them on every envelope, holding bubble hands and wearing triangular hats. Some letters wrap Polaroid images faded almost to nothing. The photographs are square and the human figures in them are diminished, like pocket fetishes. Here the Marine beams beside his F-4 Phantom, the war machine he calls the Double Ugly, on the runway at Chu Lai. And now the Marine on R&R, drunk as willows with his buddies in a Bangkok street.

Tejada knows the story.

Natalie does not regret the marriage but, given the chance, would not repeat it. *It was every cliché about the urgency of love in wartime,* she says—*seize it now or never see it again.* She barely knows the Marine when she accepts his proposal, but they are young, so young, and he is off to war.

The Marine ships out two weeks after the wedding. She takes the summer job in DC, working for her Congressman. Almost at once her husband seems an apparition. She tries to create versions of him during her nights in the library at Georgetown, prepping for grad school in the fall. She finds moments, snatches of dialogue between them, his hyper-serious look in uniform, a recruiting poster in the flesh. But she does not find an embodied person to remember and to wait for. Because they are so different she cannot imagine an inner life for him, that is part of the problem. He rarely reads, and when he does, it is *The Exorcist* or war novels by Jack Higgins. How will they talk, when he comes home?

When she answers the letters she never mentions the first time she meets Roger, or how much she was put off by him. That would be the morning he arrives for a meeting with the Congressman, splays his long hands on her desk, and quotes from a Catullus poem in Latin with his big face too close to hers. Then he asks about her studies, referencing specific texts she has checked out in the library! How would he know that? After Roger passes through to the Congressman's office, the legislative counsel, a man named Pledger who moves as if he's stalking something, approaches her and whispers as though they have a secret.

How do you know him?

I don't know him at all, she says. But Tejada knows that isn't true. Even then, as she says it, she feels the layers of knowing.

It was Pledger who got her the job. He is friendly with her parents, who support the Congressman's campaigns. His words are taffy and his sentences are aphorisms. *Back home,* he whispers, *they teach us the difference between good snakes and bad snakes before they turn us loose. That one's poison.* The look on his face is so operatic, Natalie always has to laugh.

Roger returns to the office again and again, with no business to transact, talking literature in a way to let it be known how well-read he is, and Pledger clucks. Roger finds reasons to run into her at the lunchtime panels and the evening receptions. It is odd that he talks so little about himself, beyond what he reads and his thinking on any subject she may raise. When Pledger tells her where he works and what he does, he expects her to be frightened, but she isn't. Roger's campaign is more amusing than frightening—he is so much older, his manner is so stately, his humor so compatible with her own—and the attraction she feels is undeniable, perplexing, unlike anything before. When he invites her to a concert, she accepts.

Pledger calls her parents, and when her father visits and tries to take her home, it only drives her closer to Roger.

The first time she is in bed with him he translates the Catullus poem, the part about the thousand kisses followed by a hundred and the hundred followed by a thousand, until the kisses can't be counted. A few weeks later they are in the same bed, in the apartment she rents in Reston, when the knock comes at the door. She answers in a bathrobe. The Chaplain with the gray, accusing eyes stands there. His mouth will say *shot down, Haiphong, officially missing in action.* Officially the way he says it always means dead. He will ask to come in and Natalie will say no and shut the door. In the bedroom, Roger is still and contained and polite, like a well-mannered boy. He doesn't need to know what happened at the door. He dresses, says he is sorry, leaves. Six months later he shows up, can never tell her where he's been. The pattern continues the whole time she is in grad school, while she writes her dissertation, and long after. One time when he shows up, he says he already knows all he needs to know about her, because he has seen what she is like when she betrays someone. That time they marry.

Natalie will not like the story told this way, Tejada says. *And there is worse to come. I should shape this part for her.*

Yes, the Marine is shot down. And the news comes as even more of a burden than it would be under the best of circumstances, because Natalie has long had second thoughts about the marriage. She sees how she was pressured into it by every aspect of her upbringing, by her parents' transparent belief that this was the storybook marriage for her, even if the storybook lived more in their minds than hers. And by her youth, and his, and by the old story of the soldier on his way to war. So many things conspired to run her down a maze and trap her! She agonizes over it. It is the most difficult thing she has faced to that

point in her life, but finally she writes a letter breaking it off, telling the
Marine she will file for the divorce, will make it easy for him, take care
of all details. Telling him how he is not to blame, how she feels like,
may even be, the worst person living in the world. She holds the letter
in her hand when the Chaplain arrives at the door.

An unlikely melodrama, Tejada thinks, but still.

In this telling Roger comes much later, after Natalie takes her TA
job at Princeton, discovers the young Tejada, and makes him her own.
There is an intense but erratic courtship that involves Catullus, she
marries Roger in a hurried ceremony her parents refuse to attend, and
they establish their first household in a big Victorian on P Street in
Georgetown, nurturing careers and entertaining those who matter on
occasions that are rare because both husband and wife are so often
away. They support one another, and provide comfort when needed.
When they are together, they often speak of her career, but never of
his. Years go by—harmonious ones for the most part—Roger retires,
and she accepts the endowed chair at Texas, where Roger enjoys the
fact that there is little winter.

Tejada has been waiting for Roger to wake up. Finally Natalie appears
and stands above him on the deck.

My God, Roger!

Roger squints into his wife's face, floating above him in the too
bright sky like a beautiful balloon.

*You didn't hear me? When you weren't in bed I thought you'd gotten
up early and gone out. But your car is here and I've been calling you, looking everywhere. Did you have that much to drink? You really frightened
me. I had a picture of you floating face down in the pool!*

A dismissive wave beneath her.

*No, really. The way you looked last night when the returns came in
from North Carolina and Pennsylvania?*

I might contemplate assassination, he says, yawning. *But suicide is a bit self-defeating.*

A beautiful, smiling balloon. Natalie is relieved to find Roger's humor intact.

There's tea, she says. *Take your time and come up when you're ready. I've got some work to do.*

That could only mean Mr. Tejada awaits at the keyboard, to be examined and adored in his every semicolon. Natalie assembles a stack of plates and gathers the stems of three wine glasses between her graceful fingers. Roger watches as she disappears from view.

Buenos días a todos, he says, to the tree limbs above him, to the bright flash of a jay streaking through his field of vision to its daily business. *Good to see the world still standing.*

Here is a new thing to know about Roger, Tejada writes.

Morning and evening, he prays for forgiveness and that the damage he has done in his life will be healed. He prays for the healing of the human-damaged earth. As a patriot born to duty, he also prays for his country. He does not feel assured of God or of the utility of prayer. His kneeling and the words he offers silently are a hopeful practice, but he is prepared to see the prayers as a ritual for his own comfort, and himself as a futile actor in a comedy.

Roger unfurls from the deck chair in gradual stages, first one limb and then another, putting effort into every motion. He winces, sits with his feet planted until he has gathered his balance, pushes himself up with a groan he catches in his throat, takes in a long breath with head thrown back and arms outstretched, and bends carefully into a down dog posture. This leaves him dizzy. Age has made the world a liquid place for him, through which he stumbles and, so far, recovers. For the most part, he accepts the conditions of aging in good humor. He clears a space between two of the abandoned bar tables and kneels with difficulty, his face reflecting the cool rays of the sun that has risen high enough to strike the pool. Toward the end of the prayer he tacks on a new addendum directed against the forces threatening the institutions that are as close to sacred as anything he knows. He struggles with the words. Is it thy will be done? Is it evil he prays against, or human nature, or the cycles of history, rolling like waves on an incoming tide?

Tejada chooses not to reproduce a text of Roger's prayer. Prayers and all, Roger remains a character Tejada mistrusts, but some things should remain private.

Upright and moving up the stone path of the walk, Roger admires the slant of daylight catching fire on the lawn, the lush barriers of loquat and swamp lily and elephant ear, the perfect harmony of colors in the flower beds. Natalie's doing, via the bent backs of the landscape crew to whom she communicates her will.

Tejada watches as Roger enters the house through the patio door, follows as he takes in the familiar objects and the spacious order with due appreciation. The detritus of last night's party has largely disappeared. For a wonderful moment he forgets that there has been a party, or why. The blooms of the orchid on the table by the cathedral window offer themselves for admiration. A long wall of books wait on their shelves, meticulously ordered. Again, Natalie's doing. He has often been away while she created these spaces they would share. But pleasant as it is in her creation, he will not become accustomed to permanent residence in this one place, nor to being sealed away from the atmospherics of the world, as an impotent witness. Yes, he could still contribute, and he is needed now more than ever. His retirement is a life sentence with no possibility of parole.

In the days when he returned from travels, there was such accord between them it sometimes seemed that they were one. That must be why they call it making a life together, this entity two people may bring to consciousness and parent, which presents its own careful face and its stipulated ways of thinking, this daemon that may be wise or foolish, may periodically lose traction and perish or recover. The entity he and Natalie nourish is a survivor, he believes, cunning even in its present domesticity, finding ways to reimagine pasts and futures and feed on scraps of common passions in the present.

He takes the staircase as an exercise, two steps at a time, with a hand on the bannister and a pain in the right leg. Once it was three steps at a time. Upstairs, he shaves and bathes and dresses methodically: a shirt crisply starched, a suit and tie and wingtips shined to mirrors. He descends, calls out a goodbye to Natalie, and closes the door. In the car, he drives with the windows down.

Natalie feels the pressure of her deadline, and her morning is getting away. Crossing the dining room on the way to her office, she sees it again. A flash of something moving, or not moving—standing. Or does not see it. Feels it with a chill. It is more an aftermath of vision than a figure, involving a curtain and a pot plant. And nothing, when she really pays attention. Nothing there at all.

Tejada rarely knows exactly what will happen. Sometimes it is revealed to him when a character breaks form or an event intrudes to redirect the action, when the foundation of things shudders and a sudden rift reveals an underworld.

Roger stands in line at a bank counter, dressed like one above it all and positioned there too, looking down on tops of heads. In front of him are two construction workers and a nurse in green scrubs, behind him a telemarketer on lunch break and a tattoo-drenched biker. He carries a deposit slip and a pair of checks endorsed with a fountain pen, never a ballpoint. A poster on the wall advises him to take advantage of the app the bank supplies, to make life easy and these tedious excursions into the analogue world unnecessary. He will not. If watchers wish to follow him, they will have to trail footprints, not keystrokes and clicks.

Nothing about the situation is unusual. No one is in the least disturbed. Each citizen present appears satisfied to own an equal share of a quotidian moment. The lobby scene is a replay of the one the day before and the day before that. What election? Nobody seems to have gotten the word that an earthquake has been followed by a tidal wave, and everything has ended. It is nothing Roger hasn't seen before, but those were other countries, far from home.

Does Roger feel unmoored in this moment? Tejada wonders. What has come over him?

Have you noticed, your country has been taken from you, Roger thinks, or says aloud? Heads swivel in the lobby. The nurse, who has just stepped before a teller, turns all the way around to face the tall, not at all unpleasant or unhinged-appearing old gentleman in the tailored suit. The security guard takes one step forward from his place at the door. *May be time to wake up and smell the coffee,* Roger tells the room. He says in a voice he knows they all can hear, *May be an hour past time.*

A motorcycle passes on the street, penetrating the silence that has dropped like a curtain in the room. A young woman appears at Roger's elbow and helps him to a small private office where she closes the door. Her name tag says Branch Manager, Ernestina Perez.

Can we call someone for you? She asks.

Her face is kind. Roger turns from it to read his own name beside Natalie's on the deposit slip.

I'm sorry, he says, and makes a waving gesture toward the lobby. *It's not their fault. That thing they elected is only the dragon. It's the ground that's giving way. The Chinese say, you know, the dragons sleep inside the mountains. You can kill the dragon, but the mountains are still falling.*

She puts a hand on his left arm, a pressure he can barely feel. *It's okay,* she says, *it's going to be okay.* She shakes her head and asks again if she can call someone.

He hands over the deposit.

Natalie sits at the keyboard in her home office. The window in front
of her looks out onto a balcony above the pool. Though it is there, the
pool is invisible and so is the ravine and the place where the homeless
camp. In the far distance she can see the downtown towers of the city,
like stones set upright for some purpose lost in time.

The intelligence of Tejada's characters, she types, *is both anticipatory
and retrospective. They are conscious of the story that is being told about
them. They experience the text just as they experience the world of the
story, which they take on faith as super-saturated with meanings they are
at a loss to interpret. Those meanings cannot be expressed as the "content"
of a particular subjectivity. Rather, the text itself becomes the meaning as
it works to form a structure of a singularly radiant and revelatory kind.
Meanwhile, as they observe the structure under construction, the characters learn that all possibilities exist for them at every moment, making
them both more free of and more constrained by the story they inhabit. I
say more constrained by because unlimited possibilities, as Tejada's people
learn to live among them, can be a daunting thing.*

In their correspondence, Tejada has told her he is fascinated by her
insights into his work, even if they sometimes make his head spin. As
he reads over her shoulder, he is surprised to see the Marine appear beside her, standing there in his dress blues, this first time and every time.
Natalie can almost see him clearly, at the edge of her vision. When she
looks at him directly he grows less and less substantial, a shape whose
outlines fail to appear. He is much smaller than in life—about the size,
Natalie thinks, of her nephew who has just started second grade—as
though death has taxed him and taken its portion. Still, the uniform
fits perfectly. The face is impassive. She knows without question that
he comes from their wedding, from the courtyard crazed with azaleas,
the arc of drawn sabers above them, the tap of one saber on her gowned
ass and the voice saying *Welcome to the Marine Corps.* Don't be sur-

prised if that happens, he had told her. It's tradition. He is forever then and she is whatever now becomes.

Nothing about the ghost is threatening. She is not frightened, and wonders why, but she cannot imagine what to say. *Let's go outside,* she finally offers. *It's beautiful out there.*

She sits on a white iron chair at the table on the balcony, beside the blooms of sweet alyssum in a planter, but he prefers to stand. He does not speak. Because of his size, she has to resist the impulse to offer him candy or an ice cream.

You know, she says, *for such a long time I felt I'd murdered you.*

His unreadable expression does not change. Why has he come? To seek an accounting? To forgive? She lets time pass. She decides, based only on a feeling, that he is not here for apologies or explanations, and she offers none. Then she realizes that she understands him as she never has before, as if his true being is only now on display in front of her, transparent and silent. *Why couldn't I know you this way when you were alive?* She asks him, and he has no answer. *Why do we need all these words?*

After a while she is acclimated to his presence, and she returns to her work. He stands beside her, more like a small sentinel than a companion.

Driving home from the bank, Roger crosses a border. The street in front of him is familiar but foreign. He has lost contact with the way. His left hand will not grip the steering wheel. He is aware of scraps of thought, loose and scattered and floating like ash in the aftermath of an explosion. He works to connect one scrap with another, but none make sense together and none can be held beyond an instant. Grasping at them makes them disappear. He feels sure there are stories in the thoughts, encrypted or shredded. It is critical to understand the stories. Are they the subtexts of his life? Are they the keys to all he has always hoped is hidden behind the curtain of the world? The moment brims with significance. The smallest things contain the largest. But enemies are close and watching. The outcome depends on him, as always. Is he up to the task? Out there, he recognizes a gauzy kind of sunlight, and spots figures both stationary and moving. But the road and the surrounding cars are no more meaningful than the sidewalks and the specters gliding on them and the facades of structures rising up at what must be the edges. Illusion, all around him. Behind it another layer of the same? Or the emptiness he has always feared most, reaching out forever? An impact jars him. Struck by an incoming shell, the car has stopped moving. Another car is joined to the front of it, in a senseless way. People appear at the windows, shouting revolutionary slogans in a language Roger cannot place. He reaches beneath his coat but he has been disarmed. He needs to study the texts.

Roger's been in an accident! Natalie punches off the phone. *They say he's had a stroke.* The Marine stands at attention. His expression does not change. Natalie grabs up her purse and dashes to her car. Her Marine waits there for her, sitting in front with his seat belt unbuckled. Looking at him, Natalie sees the sunlight strike the leather of the upholstery, the open space between herself and the passenger door. The Marine stares straight ahead. Natalie wonders if he can see over the dashboard, or through it. *Oh my God, what next,* she says. *Oh my God.*

The Marine stands beside Natalie at the end of a row of chairs near the hospital's emergency entrance. She is no less concerned about Roger, no less agitated, just because her mind supplies another passage for her current work. Tejada understands how misfortune shakes the words loose. She writes on a small notepad with the hospital's name at the top.

For Tejada, a thought can be an act as real as a gunshot. Should he create a version of Macbeth, Great Birnam wood would move up Dunsinane Hill not because the trees had been cut and carried but because movement toward the usurper is immanent in the trees. And in the event that the trees do not move their non-movement would register and result in its own consequences.

Poor old Macbeth, Tejada thinks, reading the note, in his hilltop castle of delusions. He is the murderer and the victim of his own story. Remember what he says? *Who can impress the forest, bid the tree unfix his earth-bound root?* And yet it happens. These things are possible because the words to say them are possible. The wood is coming for him as it has for our Roger. Think of the lives in those trees, the insects, the bacteria and fungi, the nests of birds and squirrels, and all the desperation in their thoughts and prayers. And while you're caring for the bugs and birds, don't forget my people, running in terror from the predatory empires of Mayans and Aztecs and Spaniards, and now desperate enough in the oppression of the gangs to risk everything running to the empire of the north to be treated as inconvenient animals. Do not tell me what is real or what is possible.

Tejada loses interest in the waiting room and walks outside through the automatic sliding doors. The light of day has separated into patches. In a sunny patch, a teenage girl holds up a smart phone to take a selfie with the sign that says Emergency in the background. He desperately wants to leave this place and return to his orchard, to the quiet of another poem. But he is caught here, in a place he never chose, among people he does not understand, who cannot live without him.

The Marine begins talking when Roger is moved upstairs in the hospital, to a private room, just after the medical personnel leave Natalie alone with her husband. He does not speak aloud and his lips do not move, but Natalie hears every word. The voice tugs at her and for a second she does not know where she is. It is neither the voice of a child nor of a disembodied specter, but of a young man hungry for the next moment of life. Still, the Marine does not speak for himself, but for Roger.

Roger's eyes are closed when he says, quite clearly, *Over a barrel.* The Marine explains that the phrase refers to a situation of nuance and complexity, in a scene where no one can be trusted. Roger does not stir. One of the monitors attached to his body beeps.

Natalie is desolate as she takes in the full impact of all that has happened. It has been so sudden. There across from her is a shell of Roger, a stuffed-doll Roger attached to cords and tubes and devices as though he belongs to them and not to her. Her only companion in this nightmare is a transparent visitor the size of a child, come from a past so distant it seems a fiction. And Tejada is behind it all! She cannot fathom this betrayal! She has been so faithful, so devoted, has loved Tejada in that pure way of one seduced by words, and thought of herself almost as a partner in his work. And this is the life he creates for her?

You cold-blooded bastard! she spits out bitterly. She knows he is watching and will have nothing to say in reply. Tears flow, and she stands to look around the room for a tissue. She becomes a child in the house in Savannah, listening through a door to her mother scream about her father's infidelities. She paces past the Marine and back to the other side of the bed, sniffling. She is ashamed to be so pathetic.

You don't like what happens? Tejada writes. *I do have something to say. Please hear me out. You, who are as good as anyone at finding complications, will know it's complicated. But do you know that once when our Roger was off on his travels he moved as a deniable phantom among the death squads in my country's civil war? Do you know he drank coffee with the colonel in charge while they tortured me in the next room? I was nineteen. Roger was approaching middle-age. His career, as they say, was in the ascendant. To him I was just one of the protesters picked up in the sweep at the university. He has no idea we are connected in this way. Complicated? Yes. It's easy to presume that Roger despised the man across from him, despised himself, but clung to the thought that he was holding the line against the end of your country's beautifully imagined freedoms. Sometimes ends come in unimagined ways. And how about you, observing the same tortured world Roger traveled through the gauze of my stories and the insulation of your tenured post? You now find yourself inconvenienced by a first encounter with a despot. But if there is an existential threat, it is only to your sense of privilege, not your flesh and bone.*

He softens, watching her bereft expression. She is vulnerable, and her situation is difficult.

Why not look at it another way? he writes.

Look at it as an inevitability, she thinks. She has long operated on the outskirts of Tejada's enterprise, in ways beneficial to them both, and now she knows what it is to be invited in. Of course this would happen. Of course she consented to this, and all that comes with it. She looks at Roger, unconscious on the bed. What Tejada says is surely possible. But would Tejada lie to her, just to watch how she reacts? She decides she will not react at all, and see how that suits him. She accepted long ago whatever Roger may have done.

She goes to the bedside and leans close. *Can you hear me, sweetheart?* She asks.

Tea kettle, Roger says.

Natalie turns to the Marine, who stands in parade rest position near the window.

You don't want to know, he tells her.

Natalie has a bed brought in and sleeps in the hospital room. She puts aside her work for several days, then picks it up without enthusiasm. It is something to do. And now, for what it's worth, she has a new perspective on her subject. At hourly intervals she stops to read to Roger or switch on news channels as a way to hold him to the world. The commentators endlessly repeat themselves, selling the anxiety of the election and its aftermath the same way they sell hurricanes. Natalie sticks to the more liberal channels, though she knows Roger followed them all, and the web sites and tweets and blogs and the papers, looking for his patterns. She grows exhausted with the news, and tries to tune it out. She sometimes blames the malignant ignorance of the voters, the fact that so many actually seem to *value* ignorance, for what has happened to Roger. The election and the stroke and Tejada's treachery reside together, in a single toxic cloud that surrounds them.

Roger dozes under the influence of the drugs he has been given, sometimes waking fitfully, a little wild-eyed but still within the boundaries of his accustomed levelheaded tone, with fragmentary comments and questions that come from beyond this room, sometimes in English, sometimes in Spanish, sometimes in German or another language. The Marine interprets from his place at the window. Natalie has given up asking him to relax and sit down. He does not respond to anything other than the words that come from Roger. Behind him in the distance there is a football stadium and, closer, a parking garage. In the morning brightness, a lineless outline defines his small body, divided by a window frame. Through the upper body, the scene outside is clearly visible, neither dimmed nor distorted. Through the lower body Natalie sees a gray wall and an electric outlet that holds the plug for a floor lamp.

One day Natalie brings in a pomegranate. Roger has always waxed poetic about the beauty of the crimson fruit and the way it is packaged and partitioned like the eggs of a new race of beings, secreted inside an enigmatic shell. She opens the skin and when he comes awake she brings a section of the fruit close to him and holds it up to his eyes in red-stained fingers.

For the first time since the stroke, he seems to fully recognize her. He smiles.

I'm trying to work out what it means, he says.

This is Tejada's story, she says. *I suppose it could mean anything. But for the present moment, we'll say it only means what it is, and call it a pomegranate.*

Pomegranate, the Marine says.

Roger studies the room. It is strange and familiar.

Would you like to catch up on the news? Natalie asks.

She switches on the television. Protest marches, the screen switching from one city to another. A million people in the streets, the commentators say.

A year passes, and the couple adjusts to a new kind of life. Roger has regained mobility in much of his body, but is still unable to walk on his own. His thought is better ordered and his speech, while not perfect, is much improved. He can be frustrated, lashing out and even crying, but more often he is in good humor, given to a laugh or a quiet smile at jokes and memories he keeps to himself. Natalie has hired nurses to attend him, working in shifts. He prefers to be outside, sitting in a wheelchair on the deck, above the swimming pool.

Natalie looks out at him through their cathedral window. The Marine stands beside him, keeping watch. He spends more time with Roger now than her. She thinks perhaps the Marine has come to see Roger as a comrade in arms or some sort of superior officer, maybe even a father figure—who knows? This pleases her. It's good for Roger to have company, even insubstantial company. Meanwhile, the physical therapist remains optimistic about further improvement over time.

The routine of this new life is broken when *The New Yorker* publishes an inspired translation of Tejada's latest work. Though it is presented as a work of fiction, the fact that Natalie and Roger appear as characters under their own first names—with the revelations about Roger's time in Central America and the intrusions into private lives—generates a controversy that extends beyond the literary and academic communities into social media squabbles, talk shows, and the back sections of the national newspapers. With all the publicity, Tejada's next story collection is rushed into production. He is lauded as a progressive hero and a genius of originality one moment and reviled as a literary serpent the next. When the media calls, Natalie refuses to comment. Her colleagues are sympathetic for the most part, though the more jealous of them relish the high pitch of gossip that goes on behind her back. She is too angry and bewildered to contact Tejada, and he does not reach out to her.

Soon after the story is published, an annual conference on Latin American Literature and Culture invites Natalie to deliver its keynote address. The organizers hope to raise the profile of their event through what amounts to a celebrity speaker, giving what they hope will be her first public answer to the author she has championed for so long.

Natalie agonizes over the invitation—this kind of exposure does not come naturally to her. Whatever she says could be misinterpreted and make matters worse. On the other hand, the opportunity to advance her standing and career is real. One early morning an inspiration comes to her, as they do, from nowhere. She wrestles with it like Jacob with the angel, but it knows how to hurt her and it wins. She accepts the invitation. Registration for the conference sets new records.

Natalie goes to work on her speech. She will not attack Tejada or defend herself. Instead, she will present an essay defending him and affirming his choices in the new work. She will set her own unexpected *sui generis* creation beside his.

Roger squeezes her hand when she kisses him goodbye before the flight to the conference. For a moment, the empty seat beside her in the Uber makes her feel abandoned. The Marine is no longer *hers*. Perhaps that is as it should be. The trip will be stressful and she wouldn't mind having a companion, but Roger needs him more.

The conference is unremarkable until Natalie is introduced to an auditorium filled with her peers, and rises to stand at the lectern. What she does next surprises everyone in the room, most of all herself. She sets aside the speech she has practiced into mirrors and says she will read instead a printout of the e-mail she received from Tejada the night before. She reads the message slowly into the microphone, pausing between sentences.

All I can ask is that you join me in seeking understanding. I would love nothing more than to understand before I write, or to come to understanding as I write, but I do not. I do not understand. My characters enter their lives as we all do, through the workings of a kind of magic. Their circumstances await them, for better or worse, richer or poorer—fully beyond the possibility of choice. (Your Marine knows this even more than you.) They wish to feel, they beg me to feel, that their lives leave traces, that their actions resonate. But so much is hidden from them. They move like what they fear they are, randomly generated particles somehow given consciousness, blown into motion by forces and great swallowings they cannot fathom or touch. They cling to tattered, second-hand ideas about themselves, about their tribes of common belief and the arbitrary boundaries that form their families, their needs and loves and hatreds, their nations, their other sources of identity. I want so badly to enforce a coherence for them, reward them for their troubles with the currency of assurance, but I fail if I bear false witness to them, and in a sense I can give them no more than they give me. You understand the stories better than I do. Can you find a way to help me in this, even though I don't deserve it? Can you save them, save yourself and me, with a few more words? There must be more here for them, for us, more than the light of day and the darkness of night and the ever-present awareness that life constricts around them with the turmoil of the age and the troubles they inflict or suffer and the progress of the sickness they themselves have brought upon the planet. I work to exhaustion, but it is more than I can do. I try to walk inside them, to guide them like a second skeleton. I look for the miracle in what they experience, in what they offer one another, in the smallest things. I surround them with what I find, with the elaborate joinings of their bodies, the drawer holding intricately tarnished spoons, the guidance systems of the insect who lands for a moment so delicately on their skins, one miniscule beacon shining after another, and beg them to notice. So much is questionable. So much happens or does not, matters or does not.

Can you forgive me?

She does not read the last sentence aloud. At first there is silence in the hall. Then a cough. The scuffling of a shoe. One person applauds, then another, until the clapping sound rises briefly and dies out. Faces wear perplexed expressions. She hears the whispers of comments but not the comments themselves. The moderator steps to the microphone and asks if she would be willing to take questions. She says she would not. A trapezoid of light appears in the aisle beside the top rows of seats as someone pushes open a door to walk out.

The doctor has advised a change of scene for Roger. He has always loved the beach, so Natalie organizes an expedition. In the car, Roger's wheelchair rides in the back, he himself strapped in the front passenger seat. The Marine sits behind Natalie where she can see through him in the rearview mirror. It's a long ride, over three hours. They pass among bucolic scenes of plowed fields and livestock in pastures, interrupted by occasional small towns. They talk, but Roger's side of the conversation only touches the subject in tangential ways, and the talking comes to an end.

Natalie turns on the radio, for the news, more for Roger than herself. It is so familiar now, such a drumbeat, that she grows numb to it. It might as well be a story from another place and time. The partisan factions committed in their bitter faiths. The mass shootings and the racial killings. The protests put down with military force. The laughably transparent lies that half the country still accepts as gospel.

Her thoughts are interrupted by an incoming message from the Marine. He rarely needs to interpret for Roger now, but does sometimes offer insights to Roger's travels in his thoughts, within his long periods of silence.

He's standing in falling snow, the Marine says, *outside a safe house in West Berlin. Cold War. He's about my age, just out of training at Camp Peary. He's part of a team that has smuggled a defecting physicist through Checkpoint Charlie on the Friedrichstrasse. The flakes are the largest he has ever seen, wider than his hand. They fall from places empty of light, they must fall forever, just to reach this place.*

Though she has rarely heard him speak it, Natalie knows Roger is fluent in German, but he has never told her that he worked in Germany.

When exactly did you work there? She asks him. She knows the question is pointless. He will not talk about his work.

In a way I think I always have, he says.

Surprised, she doesn't know how to respond. Finally she asks, *What is it like to be there?*

Too much blood to wash away, on too many hands.

He's through talking, she can see. By now she knows the limits to his participation in the present world, and the signs that he is elsewhere. She lets him rest.

Eventually they reach the ferry that will take them to an island. Natalie unloads the wheelchair and helps Roger into it, so he can follow the passage from the deck. The Marine has joined them. If he were visible, an onlooker might take the three of them for an older couple with a strange grandchild in a military costume, out on an adventure. Gulls swarm above their heads, studying them as prospects for a crust of bread, calling to them to be sure they notice. Roger looks from the gulls' perspective at himself in the wheelchair, at Natalie beside him in her scarf and her sunglasses, at the topsides of surrounding cars. When the gulls sail off he sails with them for a while, over a marina crowded with upreaching masts, a tug boat heading out into a channel. The wind currents float his body like the gentlest water. Far below him sunlight shatters on the surface.

Worth it, the Marine says.

At the island, Natalie unfolds a blanket on the beach not far from the surf, gets Roger settled in, and lays out a picnic lunch. Natalie takes Roger's hand. The Marine stands beside them with his face to the cresting waves, ever watchful.

Nature

They gathered at Aunt Penny's. It was always an event when Skylar brought her latest. Skylar's mother Frances and her husband Buster were the first to arrive. Her father Damon came alone. Aunt Penny's husband Alejandro served the drinks.

One thing to know, Frances said, when they had exchanged the usual and settled in. *There's been a recent tragedy. His cousin, an older cousin, lost her life in a terrorist attack, in Biarritz.*

Why didn't you tell me? Penny said.

I thought I had.

A bunch of Basques, Buster said.

What do Basques have to be so unhappy about? Damon asked. He noticed the new travertine side table and the plaster maquette that might have been a Henry Moore. He had always admired Penny's taste.

Biarritz used to be a whaling town, Alejandro said. *Its coat of arms shows a whale and a whaleboat with five sailors in berets. The inscription says the air, the stars, and the sea are helping me.*

Lost her life, what does that mean? Damon said. *It rolled under a couch? She left it on a table in a bar? She got blown up and disappeared from view, is what she did.*

She was stabbed, Buster said.

What else do we know? Penny asked.

An unsettled childhood, Frances said. *Raised in an RV as the only child of a single father, rambling through the west. The man was a lepidopterist with a side hustle as a short order cook. It was all butterfly nets and spatulas. The boy had to shift for himself. The RV was haunted, according to Skylar. One night outside of Phoenix, its lights and windshield wipers came on without the intervention of a living human and it rocked from side to side when there was no wind.*

We all want agency, Penny said. *We want community.*

I like that term, Damon said. *Side hustle.*

A bell began to peal somewhere. Aunt Penny had lived in this house since 1980, when Herman Tarnower, the diet book celebrity, was murdered by his lover in a home down the way, and no one in the family had ever heard the bell.

The door opened as if on its own, and after a moment of suspense Skylar burst through the opening with a young man in her wake. Damon rose to be the first to greet them, extending his hand.

Damon, he said. *The father.*

The young man took the hand and gazed earnestly at Damon.

He's Phillip, Skylar said.

Phillip, Damon repeated. *What is it about meeting people, Phillip? Do you ever wonder, when you meet someone, if they are really there? Of course there's always the possibility that they are an illusion or an impostor, but I mean their attention may be elsewhere, and if so can they really be said to be present in the body that is shaking your hand?*

Consciousness is the narrative of the senses, Alejandro said. *An unaccountable mystery.*

Phillip was trying not to think anything. He was not especially successful. When he had this difficulty, he repeated to himself *I'm trying not to think, I'm trying not to think,* which sometimes worked. He presented himself a half-step closer to Damon, who thought he had a nice haircut, but lacked an intelligent face. When the face wanted to express interest and engagement, its brow arched up toward the haircut, dragging the eyebrows along in an inverted V and furrowing the flesh in a way that suggested constipation.

Alejandro brought drinks for the new arrivals, and all took their seats.

I can't wait to know how you met, Aunt Penny said.

Phillip studied Skylar with an anxious curiosity.

I was crossing the little wooden bridge in the preserve, Skylar said, *and a chunk of limb fell out of a tree overhead and into the stream. I kind of shrieked.* She turned to address Phillip, who was all attention. *I have a really profound startle reflex.* Phillip nodded. She turned back to the family group, seated in the front row just below the stage, and gestured at the recessed lighting in the ceiling. *I looked up and there above me was a man standing in the tree, and staring down. A disheveled man in scuffed-up hiking boots. His shirt may have been open. I said You startled me. And he said I guess life really could make a person nervous, with all the uncertainty. I was afraid he might jump out of the tree. There was nobody else in sight, until Phillip materialized at the other end of the bridge. There is something about bridges, and about people standing at the other end of them in an anticipatory way as though they have come to greet you at the end of your travels. I crossed the bridge in a hurry and went straight to Phillip. I felt I had been rescued. Then of course we walked on together and learned how much we have in common.*

Ordinary life is filled with compelling coincidence, Frances said, *though so much is pure commotion.*

You want a day that gives more than it takes, that's all, Damon added.

Penny clapped her hands together. *Meant to be!* she said.

Puts me in mind of An Occurrence at Owl Creek Bridge, by Ambrose Bierce, Alejandro said. *Except the man there is being hanged, and there's no one in a tree.*

The air conditioner clicked on. It did not make a fuss, though it had come to share with all life forms and machines a certain sense of tipping scales. The thermostat said 71 F. Outside, the atmosphere wrapped the Earth like a tattered doily.

Six Time Jimmy's last real job was the graveyard shift at the convenience store/Subway outside Comanche, Oklahoma. Jimmy liked hiking boots. The soles of the boots adhered to the tacky substances covering the store's floor and made Velcro noises as he walked. When the manager told him to mop he left a sheen of water riding like a marsh above the substances so that walking could turn to skating at any time. When the marsh dried up, insects resumed their maneuvers in bursts across the aisles like tiny Formula One cars.

The store lived on an expanse of simmering parking lot with eight indifferent gas pumps, within sight and sound of an interregional highway. The sun poured down, sometimes in benevolence but often in wrath. In the late afternoons when the angle of the sun produced a lean-to of shade along the east side of the building, and at all hours of the night during Jimmy's shift, tidy packets of powder passed from hand to hand in exchange for cash. Jimmy didn't mind the job. He was proud of the sign on the restroom door that said Please Don't Mess This Up, within a stoloniferous design of his own making.

He was Six Time because he had been charged with six felonies and never been convicted. His past enwrapped him like a robe of office, but he wore it lightly. He lost his employment when two of his homies held up the store and the manager suspected an inside job. Jimmy saw no point in denying anything. Life moves on, and he had reason to be satisfied. At that time he lived under the care and within the doublewide of a woman named Marva Collins, who had five stray dogs. He had never been more comfortable. Jimmy liked how Marva had stenciled the walls of her residence with silhouettes of prickly pear, bringing the outside inside. But now he discovered that Marva had her limits. She tired of keeping an unemployed companion in beer and candy bars and set him loose.

Farewell, rapscallion, Marva said, as he departed. She had been weighing one word against another all morning.

That stings, Jimmy said.

So be it, Marva replied. *A person must rise to the challenge to describe the indescribable.*

The rejection struck Jimmy as an ambush, it was so clearly undeserved. He had a heart as big as all outdoors. Pretty much everybody said so, his Mama and maybe others too. But the blow, as some blows can, propelled him to a life-changing turn. Jimmy had long aspired to wander cross-country and see what he could see. Now he was accountable to no one and nothing held him back. He set out on the road, untroubled by boundaries, and added volumes to his life experience. There were some misadventures, and his presence sometimes caused unwelcome ripples in the world. While sleeping on a loading dock in Tuscaloosa he was attacked by a madman wielding a two by four against his skull. It could have been the end of him, had not the man slipped on Jimmy's blood and broken his own ankle. For the first day or two in the hospital misty forms that were not nurses or doctors or not quite anything entered the room. Jimmy spoke to them but they did not speak back. Still, the stay was restful, with room service, a television, and a bill for forty thousand dollars no one knew where to send. The scar ran from his temple down to his upper jaw. The world did act a little stranger afterwards, with deeply saturated colors and occasional lightning strikes at the periphery and whispers in it or behind it Jimmy couldn't quite catch. But it had the look of something freshly made and it called Jimmy to move through it and keep moving. Like a migrating bird, he dreamed best on the wing.

At present he enjoyed the accommodations of a nature preserve in Purchase, New York, where Amelia Earhart took flight from the polo grounds. He owned a toothbrush and a sleeping bag from the

Salvation Army store in Ardmore. From nature he borrowed a mattress made of leaves and a crow's nest lookout in a favored tree. He slept by a small stream, with its lullaby inside him. Handouts provided beer money. And he was not above taking meals and the occasional shower in shelters, even when they came at the price of a homily.

Was there precarity? There was. But Jimmy knew the truth. Precarity is a condition to which no one is immune.

Skylar and Phillip went shopping. Skylar needed a new pair of boots, and the wonderful Italians, who were suddenly having so many problems, were resilient and still making boots. Skylar told Phillip about Perugia. They would go there together, as soon as the problems are over, as long as it's not still so hot. Skylar did not dither. She knew what she wanted the moment she saw it. She held just the right boots up for Phillip to admire, tried them on and they fit perfectly. Clothing and accessories can either support you or they can let you down. The boots were very supportive. *I'm going to wear them out!* She said. The clerk put Skylar's old boots into the box the new boots came in.

On the sidewalk outside the store Six Time Jimmy counted the bills and change he had collected. He was hungry and had enough to buy a meal. He could wait until evening and eat at the shelter, and meanwhile buy a six pack and a Snickers and go back to the preserve, or he could gratify the hunger with a burger that costs five times as much as a burger in Comanche. Deciding was usually easy. Today he found it difficult. Perhaps it was a quality of the light and its play with shadows on the walk that brought confusion. Perhaps Jimmy was slightly unmoored. With a start he realized how he missed his perch on the limb above the stream, like a soldier misses home. It was not that the elevation caused him to feel in any way superior there. It was the peaceful vantage on the life below, the attitude of thoughtfulness it brought, the occasional feather drifting downward, the pulse of the tree's arteries extending to the congregation of its leaves and the sensation of its musculature as it supported him, the uplifted look of his hiking boots planted on the bark between his eyes and the bridge top, the water in its humble passage. In this moment he saw no need to explore another inch of the world. The tree was the great discovery of his travels, he realized. Its roost would understand him, finally, would still the restless movements of his body and free his mind and soul. The tree was rooted. It did not need movement. A different kind of world waited in its branches, but you had to climb there. He knew the tree had much to teach him. Perhaps it could heal and redeem.

As Jimmy pocketed his money and headed out for the preserve, Skylar and Phillip exited the store, with Phillip holding the shoebox. The three of them fell into line abreast, their strides all purposeful and matching. The band moved together, but each member moved in their own envelope of being, trailing pasts behind. Six Time Jimmy forgot that he was hungry. Phillip forgot the haunted RV and the cousin he barely knew who was killed in Biarritz. Skylar forgot the old boots in the box. But now the past broke through and Jimmy remembered his Grandma. *I declare,* she used to say when he was very small. He could hear her speaking but could not remember exactly how she looked. *Well I declare.* But there were no declarations. Only many prefaces. The declarations are still waiting somewhere, until the time is right.

I do declare, he said aloud in Grandma's voice, and Skylar turned mid-step to study his profile, more than a bit alarmed. She caught a whiff of odor and a glimpse of a pirate's scar. There are after all crazy people on the streets, potentially dangerous and to be avoided. Now this one had crossed the border of her personal space and brought an eerie chill besides. Had she seen him in a dream, foretelling this perilous moment? Quickly, Skylar spread a hand on Phillip's clavicle and urged him forward, breaking up the marching line.

———

I know now, I know! Skylar told Phillip as they sipped post-purchase Frappuccinos. *The dissociated man, the man off his meds who walked beside us and said he would declare as though he were channeling a ghost. I felt we had all walked together before, impossible as that may be, in that disquieting way an event can be familiar as though it has played out in exactly the same way but in another time and place. That is what unnerved me for a moment, but now I know the truth. He is the man in the tree! The one who, when considered in a certain way, brought us together. On the one hand we owe him a debt of gratitude. On the other, now that he has presented himself to us with all his needs exposed we have an obligation, a social contract, to confront him and be sure he does no harm to himself or others. Don't you agree? We must seek him out, assess his state of mind, and if necessary notify authorities.*

Almost all nearby creation listened in on Skylar's proposition. The trees chopped into napkins and cups, the dredged-up dinosaurs compounded into plastic Starbucks logos, the migrant coffee beans ground to fragrant dust. The other customers and the barista were lost within their own concerns and had no clue. But not so far away there was an ocean, inching closer to listen and to touch.

Phillip nodded his ready assent.

This is more than we can safely manage on our own, Skylar continued. *We will involve the family.*

She called her mother, who notified Aunt Penny, and within an hour the same group that had welcomed Phillip gathered once again at Penny's house. Skylar laid out the situation in all its urgency. The endeavor was noble, clearly. As she knew they would, the family mobilized around her.

Truth be told, we are too well insulated from suffering, Penny said. *That's why no one is interested in people like us anymore.*

It's so odd that we've never discussed this, Frances said.

Who can judge? Damon wanted to know.

Fate assigns our roles, Alejandro added.

They traveled in four cars, as a convoy. There was security in numbers. Their mission was stimulating, whether anyone said so or not. From the parking area they moved as a tight group along the nature trails, in a determined silence.

From his crow's nest, Six Time Jimmy watched them coming, followed their progress as they lined up below him on the middle of the bridge. After a moment in which the universe of one and the multiverse of seven regarded and speculated upon the capabilities and interests of one another, Jimmy was the first to speak.

Can I help ya'll in some way? he asked.

You are there and we are here, Skylar replied. *How can the gap be narrowed?*

The people were not armed as far as Jimmy could see, though they might have been insane like the man in Tuscaloosa. He thought about it. About being big-hearted as all outdoors and how the tree had taken him in just as he was, without question. Finally he said *You could come up, I guess. That is if the limb will hold.*

No one moved to take advantage of the invitation.

Skylar posted an image of the scene on her Instagram page. More than a claim of identity, it was a profound record of life and time that said everything. Her new boots, already featured in another posting and thus participating in a thematic echo, entered at the bottom of the frame, overlooking the stream. At the top of the frame Six Time Jimmy sat like a jubilant prophet comfortably upon his limb, his long legs suspended as if defying gravity. Between these two elements of composition stretched the natural world, encapsulated, doomed, and promising revenge. And outside the frame, the complications without measure!

The group on the bridge offered questions Jimmy did not seem to understand, though he did appear to be studying them closely. Perhaps he was disabled in terms of his skills of comprehension, or unable to martial his thoughts. *What are your origins? What do you remember? What have you learned? To what do you attest? Do you complain? Or keep silent?*

Marva had often spoken of UFOs. She claimed to have seen spots of light above the trailer that approached her, danced and vanished. Once she had cried out *I don't like all that flying* in her sleep as Jimmy lay beside her. *They want to interrogate us and know what makes us tick,* she later told him. Perhaps Marva had spent time among the extra-terrestrials. She had certain knowledge. She hung, for example, long strips of aluminum foil from the trees around her trailer, to channel energy directly from the cosmos into the ground beneath her feet. The memory made Jimmy more curious about these beings on the bridge and their activities, and about his own perceptions of them. For example, they receded from him as they asked their questions, becoming farther away. The distance seemed to go on forever.

The inquiries gradually dwindled, and in the absence of voices the stream could be heard trickling in another language beneath the suspended actors in the scene. Finally Damon gestured with outstretched palms at his companions.

Stalemate, I'd call it, he said. *Back to the house for drinks?*

With last looks upward and a certain air of resignation, the family began moving back the way they'd come. But Phillip hesitated.

I'll go up, he said.

All eyes turned his way in some surprise.

Down the bridge and up the tree he climbed, with dexterity and purpose. All watched him closely, especially Jimmy, who reconsidered the invitation to join him on his limb. But when Phillip slipped a bit and might have fallen, Jimmy extended a hand to help him with the final step. There was nothing alarming about the young man's grasp. Up close, he looked harmlessly vacant. They settled down together.

Phillip, Skylar called, *come down.*

From his new perspective, Phillip gazed steadily at the group on the bridge, his eyebrows lifting into his look of concentration, but he did not come.

———

Phillip had always found that not thinking anything made him feel comfortable. In that way, not thinking anything was like air conditioning. When one is comfortable within, one can go anywhere, thrive in any habitation. Sometimes though, no matter how comfortable it was, not thinking anything could kind of seep into its own foundation and get slippery and slide down a hole. Phillip took care to stay away from the edges of the hole. He had certain techniques for doing this. He followed strict routines. He brushed his teeth in the same order every morning, upper outside upper inside lower outside lower inside. He never looked at any one thing too long because objects too long regarded tended to violate the law of inertia, moving unpredictably when still or stopping when in motion as if they knew they were observed. He never visited a place that was too much like a place he had visited before, to spare himself the trap of compulsion to compare and contrast. He tried to avoid saying things that everyone already knew, though that was among the hardest tactics of all. Mostly it required staying silent.

Now, from his new position on the tree limb, he felt he had left his thoughts below, that his thoughts had in some way departed with the people on the bridge, who after a brief period of echoing Skylar's call and receiving no response had gone away. The stream moved on below. It had never stopped, never paused. Dappled sunlight struck golden sparks on it that burst into nothing as though that was their only business in the world. He sat beside Six Time Jimmy, their shoes dangling in the way of comrades.

If you're hungry later we can get dinner at the shelter, Jimmy said, and Phillip nodded.

Time passed, or re-arranged itself, especially for Jimmy and also especially for Phillip and for all the people who had once stood on the bridge, but made no spectacle of passing. Jimmy showed Phillip the best way to climb down, and then showed him how to build sailing craft of twigs with leaves attached as sails. They held regattas on the stream. The sailing made it easy for Phillip to not think anything.

Skylar checked her Instagram feed that night. Her post had already drawn 105 Likes, the most since the video of herself crying. The comments were enthusiastic. People were noticing the heron catching just a spot of light upstream, almost mid-center between the new boots and the man in the tree. If you didn't look closely you could miss it. It didn't even seem to belong and yet once you knew it was there it became the most important thing.

Underwaterville

Facing the full moon, raise your hands into the *I surrender* position. Observe closely, to register all that comes to the surface. It is all there, always. If you need proof, just look anything that has an eye in the eye.

An illustration of the point, if one is needed. One late morning Chapa walked through my front door as I sat on the humpbacked couch studying a cat's eye marble I had found under a dresser and weeping. I never locked the doors. I reasoned that if a thief broke in, I might have to add to my losses the cost of repairing the door along with anything the thief might fancy. There was not much to be had, and what there was belonged to the landlord. The marble looked back at me via its unspeakably beautiful and numinous eye.

Sometimes I weep not because of any single grief, I told Chapa, *but just because I need to. I tell you this so we can know each other better.*

Land O'Goshen, Chapa said. He had just encountered the phrase and found it magnificently strange. For him, it said everything about Anglos. Chapa had wonderful teeth. He wore the badge of his profession on a strap around his neck—a battered Pentax camera with a zoom lens and a flash attachment, loaded with 35mm film. The digital world was the Ghost of Christmas Yet to Come.

Earlier that morning I had been released from jail, following a piddling charge that involved swimming naked in a prophet's stock tank. There was moonlight on the full. There was air like overheated soup in the Texas summer. Breathing underwater was more comfortable. When I came up through the surface and stood nipple-deep facing moonward, with an unaccustomed sense of palpable existence—though how hopeful could it be to find oneself attached by no more than corporal gravity to a minor toy of gods that spins and blows across the heavens headed who knows where—the mud of the scooped-out bottom squished between my toes, and remained there as a solid aggregate inside my socks as I sat on the metal bunk in my cell. The moon has gravity too.

I lived in a small house that some years past had been stamped out by a great house-stamper running up and down the rows of streets to plant identical houses on tiny lots in what passed for a suburb, though the town was too small to accommodate a proper suburb, marketed to those who could not afford better. The local real estate market had collapsed due to a drought that lingered in an already dry part of the world. Half the houses on the street had been up for sale, and then offered for rent at bargain basement prices once they failed to sell. Because the houses looked so much alike, people were always coming home to the wrong place, making honest mistakes. A nice young couple, the Does, Jane and John, lived next door. They were immigrants, I don't know from where. Occasionally I caught a glimpse of Jane standing at their picture window, waving good-bye to John as he drove off to work. All the houses had a picture window. Jane wore a kitchen apron. Sometimes I wondered what had become of the house-stamper. Was it obsolete and unemployed? Was it all alone? Had it stamped its own grave in a landfill?

I worked then for an endangered species, a weekly newspaper. It means little to say so, since everything's endangered now. But at that juncture the danger was still over the horizon, far out past the breakers and the looming promontories. You couldn't find it with a telescope, but it was there. I was the investigative reporter. Not many weeklies had investigative reporters, but that's what it said in my byline.

I arrived on a bus to interview for the job, and hailed what I later learned was the town's only cab. The ride took no more than a minute to pass the whole of downtown, where many of the businesses stood shuttered and empty, like missing teeth. At the newspaper I asked for the person who had responded to my application, the Editor and Publisher, and followed one of the few employees through a narrow cinder block structure to what turned out to be the only office on the premises worthy of the name. By which I mean it had its own walls and door. The employee knocked in the most tentative and fearful way. A growling sound that could have been a word emerged. Opening the door, I found the Editor and Publisher, a woman whose family had operated the paper for four generations, sitting at an overburdened desk. This woman, I would learn, was known to all persons as the E&P.

What's your name? She asked as I stood in the doorway.

I told her.

As long as it's not Arledge, she said. *Do you know any Arledge's? Do you have any in your bloodline? Related by marriage or cousins once removed or any of that?*

I said no to all the above. Then I remembered that Roone Pickney Arledge Jr. was a revered network executive who ran both sports and news at ABC, and I said that.

This soured her noticeably.

So you do know one, she said.

Not personally, I said.

I filled the ensuing silence by handing across my resume. I had made an earnest effort on the document and thought it historically accurate as far as it went. It told of stops at big city dailies, a capitol bureau, news services, even major market TV, plus a short list of awards. It did not go into detail on the awards. It seemed unnecessary to mention that they were shared with others, for the most part with entire staffs of others. The stops were all brief, but what is the real experiential difference, beyond a quantity of passing seconds, between a moment and a lifetime? I had long ago accepted this career trajectory that some might judge as a freefall. A mayfly lives 24 hours at best. The brevity factor, as I saw it, was far outweighed as a consideration by the sheer number of the stops, a near-Homeric list of mayfly lifetimes. In any case, as a record of my own life and work the resume was laughably inadequate. Each of the stops it mentioned represented many stories I had written down, and each of the stories was a failure because each left out what I didn't understand, which was mostly everything. From a journalistic perspective, it must be said, the stories did record the Who What When Where of particular situations. The Why went missing on the page. There was always something underneath or hidden behind I couldn't get to. Always the essential part, I knew, the untold, key-to-understanding part abandoned and calling out to me, like an orphan.

The final section of the resume consisted of five professional references, a substantial number. I had persuaded all the people listed there to lie on my behalf. I found it was not really hard to persuade people to lie once they know you've been reduced to applying for a job on a weekly in a remote Texas town. Pity comes into play.

The E&P tossed the resume back across her desk after only a summary glance.

I don't like the name Arledge, she said.

I wondered how to describe her face. Then I wondered if I should apologize on behalf of all Arledge's, past, present, and to come, even though I'd never met one. I ended up nodding and shuffling in place. I find there is no one way of standing that is completely satisfactory. She had not offered me a chair. I didn't feel mistreated because there was no chair besides hers. She picked up a nearby sheet of copy and began reading it in a distracted way. This gave me a chance to decide that the sharp planes of her face were somewhat like a chunk of flint half-shaped into a weapon, and somewhat not. Though seated she was clearly an exceptionally tall woman, with blunt hands that looked strong. She wore bifocal glasses in cat eye frames clamped onto a delicate chain that looped down her back to keep the glasses handy. She leaned in close to the paper, curving her back in a striking arc. I worried about osteoporosis. Her hair was long and straight, in the style once favored by female folksingers and fashionably conforming male nonconformists. It parted to expose an ear too small for the head it grew from.

Look at that shit, she said, launching the copy sheet my way.

I picked up the paper and did as I was told. Certainly all narratives are bald-faced lies, but this one had an unpretentious charm. It was a solemn, if uninspiring, item about a local car dealership—Savage Autos—acquiring another dealership in a nearby town. The acquisition would expand the company's holdings in the area to a modest empire of three store fronts. There were no misspellings. The lede was clear and unburied. Quotes were attributed to a source. The sentences were constructed in accord with conventional grammar, and adequately saturated with the illusion of linear time. The reporter, one Becky Untergarten, came before her reader, spoke the Who What When Where and even the supposed Why of the situation, and stepped back into the darkness without elaboration. The story did glorify the way a local business prospered in hard times, without mentioning that expansion could be relatively painless for any well-funded enterprise when competitors were folding on all sides. In sum it was the kind of article one expects to find on page one of a small town weekly, the kind I would no doubt be expected to write were I so fortunate as to land the job.

Do you see it? The E&P asked, with impatience, when I set the copy paper down.

I considered and rejected several answers. This took too long.

You fucking don't! And it's right there in front of you! She yelled. I may have jumped back a half step. *Do you know who the Savages are?* *That's a question that has long interested me,* I said. *I suspect they're not who most of us think they are.*

Exactly! She said, suddenly mollified. *You saw that one right away. You may be the man for the job!*

She pushed the glasses upward on her nose and looked directly at me for the first time. I wondered what she saw. In the mirror, I sometimes looked like an experiment gone wrong. While I had become an object of interest, not always a good thing in my experience, she seemed in search of confirmation of a positive impression, as opposed to a reason to have me thrown out.

I wonder if the Savages are connected somehow to the Arledge's, I ventured, striking an attitude of cool inquiry.

She snapped her fingers and pointed at me. Then she pulled back the thumb on the pointing hand like the hammer on a pistol and let it fall.

Monty Arledge snuck in that back door and married Tom Savage's daughter, she said. *Knew exactly what he was doing. He doesn't love that woman. Who could? He was after something else, and by God he got it. That's the oldest story in the book, you're thinking. But that doesn't scratch the surface.*

Follow the money, I said knowingly.

Yeah, that's the surface, she said. *But by God it's a place to start.* She gave me a coy wink. I have always felt ambivalent about facial expressions. It turned out the wink meant I was hired. My salary was sufficient to support a family of four small birds. The E&P did not offer a handshake or welcoming small talk. She searched the desk until she found a business card from a real estate agent who advertised in the paper, and handed it across. I rented the first place the agent showed me, next door to the Does.

Have you ever known bone-deep that you were on the wrong track but been unable to jump off or stop the train? Or to dress a less personal but tangential question in a metaphor more in keeping with stock tanks under moons, what powers these currents of inevitability? The structures of the muddy bottom beneath us are too intricate, too hidden, to imagine. They cannot even be called structures. This is why one surrenders.

I received my assignment the morning of my first day on the job. I say *my assignment* as opposed to *my first assignment* because there was only one: The Arledge Story, with a scope of guaranteed employment that extended until *every filthy crumb, every snake-hole* had been investigated and exposed *down to the packed dirt floor.* What might happen after that was unclear. I would have priority access to Chapa, the staff photographer, anytime I needed him, taking precedence over his already crowded schedule of livestock auctions, bankruptcy hearings, and bake-offs. I asked the E&P if she had any suggestions as to a more specific focus for the Arledge series.

Oh, I've got plenty of suggestions, she said, *but I'd rather see what you come up with. Eyes wide open, ear to the ground. Go. Go. Go!*

I moved what there was to move into my new abode and began to get my bearings in the town. There is a reason they say first impressions matter. My first impression was that the town worked like an ant mound, obsessed with itself and its desperate purposes. It was also concerned with the elimination of the unusual and the disruptive. I saw few stray dogs. I was treated as a stranger, which is to say I was barely treated at all. To overcome this problem and also to eat when hungry, I presented myself regularly at a café called the Blue Moon, which served as the center of the mound. The Moon, as it was known, offered hearty if not healthy breakfasts, an all-you-can-eat lunch buffet, and an exotics-free dinner menu with a nightly special. Meat loaf night drew the biggest crowds.

I am always ready to admit that, in a given group, I may be the one who is, as my mother used to say, *not quite right.* This is the first and simplest explanation when any situation teeters off into the strange. There is, though, an upside to my social disadvantage. My not quite rightness tends to push me to the edge of things, where I can observe and report with a measure of objectivity. From my position in a Moon booth, I studied local patterns of association and communication. Subtle head nods were popular among males, as a way of acknowledging one another. Most of the heads wore large cowboy hats made of straw, which accentuated the nodding action. I came to think of this gesture as the Nod of Belonging. It said *I see you there and I accept your presence. Probably I will not do anything terribly violent to you at this time, although I could.*

Females were more demonstrative. They tended to raise their hands and wave broadly as though they stood on the opposite side of an open field. Often they followed the wave by crossing the room to converse. These processes were fairly reliable, and the faces of the diners began to be familiar. There was only one digression from the norm, when a clutch of women who looked like refugees from the nineteenth century appeared at the take-out counter, gathered up an impressively large order in the course of several trips to and fro, and drifted away. Their skirts almost dragged the floor. Their long-sleeve blouses buttoned to the neck in an over-abundance of modesty—not, in my opinion, the best choice considering the searing temperatures outside—and two of them wore antique bonnets on their heads. When I asked the waitress who they were, she said they were the Prophet's people. I asked who the Prophet was and she said it was none of her business in a way designed to tell me it was none of mine.

A few meals in the place brought an illusion of progress. The waitress had begun to smile in an amused way as she took my order, and once when I tried nodding at a man he nodded back, after an uncomfortable delay that made it clear he knew I had never worn a cowboy hat. I practiced my Nod of Belonging in a mirror. It was difficult to perfect. Too small a nod was imperceptible. A larger nod seemed necessary to compensate for the lack of a hat, but too large a nod looked narcoleptic. Café patrons often spoke among themselves and then turned collectively to look my way, like birdwatchers sighting a rare species.

But then a new edition of the newspaper appeared, with a bold page one headline that said *Investigation Begins*. The Becky Untergarten story was short on specifics but long on promise. It spoke of *long-buried irregularities* and *corrupt practices* that would be *brought to light*. Alongside a head shot credited to Chapa, where I evaded eye contact with the lens, I was introduced as the decorated, veteran journalist in charge of light-bringing. My more impressive career stops and awards had been lifted from the resume and set out in a sidebar in the form of a bulleted list. Becky Untergarten was an eager young woman with powder blue fingernails. I envied her. She interviewed me for the story and kept trying to get a useful quote, but I'm afraid I wasn't much help. She resorted instead to a series of quotes from the E&P, to the effect that *the unprincipled malefactors who so long have run roughshod* in the community were now *on notice*. People began to avoid me like mosquitos avoid a garbage fire. No matter where I settled in the Moon, an empty circle quickly developed around me. In the local grocery, shoppers became deeply interested in their carts or their own footwear when they spotted me coming toward them down an aisle.

One day I invited Chapa to join me for lunch. He brought his own flatware—a knife, fork, and spoon wrapped in a cloth napkin along with a toothbrush and a traveler's size tube of Colgate toothpaste. Without my asking, he explained that he had once contracted food poisoning after a meal at the Moon and that he was suspicious of its dishwashing practices. I hoped he might provide some insights on the town. Instead, he introduced me to one of his many theories, the one about clouds. Chapa believed that well-formed cumulus clouds of the type prevalent above the town in summertime are provided as a test of human intelligence. No one could interpret an entire cloud message in all its complexity, he said. That was no more given to us than any of the fundamental purposes of existence. But rare individuals could tease out a bit here and there. For instance, the shape of a bear's paw dissolving into the suggestion of a wing and closely followed by another cloud in the form of a sleeping lion might, according to his own interpretation, suggest that a united and peaceful world was possible but not before humans leave the scene. Proper cloud reading required an openness to intuitive leaps, Chapa maintained. There were so many available messages and so many potential interpretations that axiomatic understandings were impossible. In any event, when clouds provided information it was never personal and never in answer to a question, as in *Does so and so love me?* That wasn't the point. Chapa advised that I avoid any Moon dish made of squash.

I did not abandon all hope in the Moon. But at this point I began to question my strategy. It seemed possible that waiting for the story to find me as I sat on the cracked naugahyde covers of a booth bench among nodding, broadly waving people who shunned me like a leper could produce results, but, I realized, those results might come at some date beyond my actuarial life expectancy. It was time to face the story head on. I asked Chapa to drop me off at Savage Motors.

Monty Arledge greeted me there at the front door, as though he had expected me forever.

He was a small man who leaned forward when he walked, preceded by a small belly that hung above his belt line, with a pair of scuffed loafers on his feet. He led me to his office, indicated the chair on the visitor's side of his desk and took a seat on his side.

You sure look familiar, he said.

I felt no need to explain that he, like everyone else, had seen my picture on the front page of his local paper.

I know you, he said, brightening. *You went to high school with my sister, Mona Arledge.*

I don't recall anything like that, I said.

You did though. In my line of work, we have to remember people, names and faces. No point even showing up without it.

I've never had the pleasure of meeting your sister, I said.

I know why you won't admit it, he said. *Mona affects people that way. If you can't say something nice, don't say anything, isn't that right?*

It may be, I said, *but I don't know her.*

You dated her, didn't you?

No.

Yeah, and no wonder you won't talk about it. You're not talking about it, are you?

No, I'm not.

You're damn right. And I've got to say I respect you for that. Most of us fall short. Who is not disappointed, not so much in life, but in themselves? Who does not hope to see a different sort, a better sort, of person when they meet themselves in a mirror? Who does not wish to free themselves of all the limitations they themselves impose? Know what you need?

I wonder, I said.

A car.

He made a sweeping gesture that did not fail to take in the showroom of the building in which we sat, as well as the lot full of cars parked outside and the totality of dark matter and dark energy composing the expanding universe.

I saw you getting dropped off here, he continued, *like a nobody! And my heart just sank. A man of your caliber can't be afoot.*

I was hoping to ask you some questions, I said.

Ask all the questions you want, he said. *I don't want a customer who doesn't ask questions. I can't respect them if they don't. Tell me what the hell we would be if we didn't question this life we're dropped down into.*

Bloody womb. Blink. Hunger and need. Blink. Naked as the day. Where does that all lead? Come out here with me.

He stood up and I followed him out onto the lot. We strolled amongst the rows of cars like monarchs surveying their domain. Sunlight glinted off the chrome.

What suits your fancy? He asked.

I'm afraid I'm not much of a car person, I confessed. In truth, I hadn't needed a car in years, in the cities where I'd worked.

Most people have a dream car, he said.

I don't, I said. The cars in my dreams tended to run me over.

Well then, let's talk price, he said. *How would you describe your range?*

Somewhere between nothing and barely anything, I said.

He veered left and I followed him into the used car section. After a bit of wandering, he slapped his palm down on a colossal sedan with a slouching posture.

There's your baby! He said. *She may have seen a better day, but she's tried and true. She'll get you where you're going.*

The chrome nameplate on her face said *Mercury* and the one on her derrière said *Monterey.* She was vast and creamy yellow with an air of decaying opulence, a Rubens brought forth from a mildewed basement. There were bald spots in her paint job, flaked with rust patterns like a moth's wing. Her tires were threadbare, and she leaned to one side as though listening to something with her better ear. She was missing all her rear-view mirrors. I loved her immediately. Arledge offered to lift her hood but I declined. It seemed too personal. Under the rubber mats on her floorboard I found a series of small holes through which I could see the pavement. They clearly formed a code, like Chapa's clouds.

Because you're a friend of the family, Arledge said, *I can let her go for three hundred American dollars, which you can pay on time. I'd think less of myself if I kept a good man from the open road.*

I named her Judy.

When I took her out for drives, I removed the mats to experience the thrill of the roadway passing under, like the ever-changing fascinations of water beneath the hull of a glass-bottom boat. That was not the only way she cast a spell of buoyancy. While I hadn't driven a car in a long time, I had only once driven a boat. She was more like the boat, drifting side to side, bobbing on the waves, requiring constant, anticipatory corrections. When asking her to stop you had to let her glide toward the place where she wanted to be. It did not take long in the Texas summer to realize that she no longer conditioned the air.

As I prepared to drive Judy off the car lot that afternoon, Monty Arledge had laid his hands on the driver's door and leaned in with a look of avuncular concern.

I know she put you onto me, he said. *It's our little game. She may want to mess with me a little, but it's the Prophet she's really after. I'll give you a hundred thousand mile warranty on that hot tip, no extra charge.* He tapped the roof above my head with a knuckle in a not unfriendly way, and then he said *Good luck.*

I had the feeling Monty might be waving as I pulled away, but the absence of rear view mirrors kept me from checking to see if I was right.

Judy and I got to know each other as she took me to a phone. There I called Chapa and he agreed to meet me back at the Moon, where the coffee left over from lunch was burning to pitch on the percolators. I repeated Arledge's cryptic message and asked if it made sense to him.

Kit and Kaboodle, he said. He fiddled with the *f*-stop on his camera lens. Then he told me what everyone else already knew. Monty Arledge and the E&P were a long-time item, the worst kept secret in the town. Monty was indeed married to Tom Savage's daughter, and the scandal of his affair with the E&P, which extended back into their teenage years, generated more than enough gossip to give the lovers a gauzy celebrity, enhanced by the flammability of the relationship. The two engaged in monumental fights that were dangerous to breakable objects. Chapa offered a number of anecdotal examples. *She doused him with a pitcher of iced tea right over there,* he said, indicating a location two booths away. *Once she hired a bulldozer to chew up his lawn.* But the spats were typically followed by a reconciliation, and the lovebirds would soon be witnessed, often here in the café, making moon eyes at one another. An unusually prolonged battle was now underway, and this explained why I had not seen the pair together. Possibly, Chapa theorized, one aspect of my hiring was to serve as, pardon the expression, a tool in the ongoing war of romance. When the E&P was unhappy with Monty, he went on, she might employ me to cast aspersions on him in the pages of her paper. She could claim deniability because the words of the attack would be those of her investigative reporter. But while this might be a passing amusement for the E&P, Chapa concluded, there could be no doubt that the Prophet was the real, the ultimate, story to be had in the town. His crowd was growing and the town was not, Chapa said. This was a problem. Longtime townies like the Savages, the Arledges, and the E&P would soon be outnumbered. I tried to stop myself from imagining the amorous couple in flagrante, but I couldn't. Monty's head kept topping out somewhere around the E&P's breastbone.

This is the point at which the focus of the investigation shifted, leading to my moonlight swim in the stock tank.

To set the record straight, it wasn't that I was drunk that night, even if the sheriff's deputies jumped to that assumption like chickens on a bug. I have learned to avoid alcohol and other perception-altering drugs. Perception is already, in my opinion, not much more than loosely controlled hallucination. Why make that situation worse? No, the problem was heartburn. There is the heart that stands as the metaphor for all we desire and mostly can't have, and there is the landscape familiar to the cardiologist, the mechanical contrivance with chambers and fleshy valves. I suppose heartburn might apply in

either context, the former in an unfortunate poetic way, but in this
case it was acid reflux, thanks to the chili special at the Moon, that
wouldn't let me sleep. Some steer who didn't want to die was having
his revenge.

That afternoon Judy had carried me to the county seat, where I
learned the location of the Prophet's ranch. I bought a map at a service station and plotted the course, which involved a paved state road
followed by a gravel county road, not much more than a narrow lane.
A few hours later, with the ghost of the steer roaming my intestines, I
paced about my rented house. It was clear the balm of sleep would not
be applied. Probably that unsettled state was what drove me to a poor
decision. I thought I might reconnoiter the Prophet's turf under cover
of darkness.

Judy and I went driving. I couldn't see as much as I thought I
should through her windshield. When I stopped and got out to investigate, I found that she only had one working headlight, and that one
was pointed at an ineffectual angle toward the side of the road rather
than the middle. After that I drove slower than I might have otherwise. The full moon was helpful. The Prophet's ranch was further from
town than it looked on the map. After a series of wrong turns—roadway signs were few and far between, and I couldn't see the ones there
were well enough to read them—we made it onto the state road. More
wrong turns followed. I worried that the sun might come up before we
arrived and spoil the cover of darkness. I also worried about the gas in
Judy's tank. I hadn't added any since I met her. Her fuel gauge claimed
the tank was around one quarter full, but I didn't know if the gauge
was in working order, and the little pointer on it didn't seem to move.
We came to a sign at a turnoff and I got out to read it. It alleged that
the gravel under my feet covered the county road we wanted. Barbed
wire fences lined the mini road on both sides. An invisible owl spoke
threateningly. The Milky Way sparkled overhead. It had moved much
closer than it had ever been before, to better fight the moon for dom-

inance. A small animal scurried over the gravel and something hissed from the brush along the fence line. I got back in Judy.

Soon the road branched into two possible options not shown on the map, neither of which was named by a sign. I made an arbitrary decision and took the branch to the right.

The night was thick and sultry. I had all Judy's windows down in hope of a breeze, but none came, and we couldn't go fast enough under current conditions to drive the air through. I leaned over the wheel and squinted to get a better view of the way ahead but it didn't help. Sweat coursed down my temples and beaded on my arms. I couldn't tell if we had gone five miles or five hundred yards when I saw the hump of something off to the right, looming a little above the brush that surrounded us on both sides. We stopped and I got out. The hump was the raised bank of a stock tank. While all the stock tanks I had noticed were reduced to muddy puddles by the lack of rain, a stock tank could still mean some amount of water, and water seemed a good idea. I pulled Judy as far to the side as possible and shut her down. I climbed between the strands of wire, ripping my shirt and opening cuts along my back. The barbs on the wire were closely followed by the barbs on the brush. A prickly pear cactus stabbed my thigh, leaving tiny daggers that didn't exit the skin for days. Finally I staggered to the tank and climbed its bank. I was surprised to find it nearly full. An expanse of water reached from one side to other, wearing the face of the moon on its back. I stripped off my shoes and clothes and waded to the center, where the water reached almost to my chin. It was warm as a soil-infused hot tub, but still a comfort. I submerged and sat down on the bottom. When breath became necessary, I came up, shaking the grimy liquid from my hair.

It was then that I raised my hands in surrender to the moon. It was a few seconds past then when I noticed the three silhouettes on the opposite bank, backlit by moon rays. My brain took in what my eyes had seen and calculated that I faced three humans of varying size and shape, each pointing what appeared to be a large gun in my direction. I left my hands where they were.

He is not of the Fold, I heard one of the silhouettes say.

You're in the Prophet's water, said another. *Get out and come here.*

I did that, though it took a minute to unstick my feet from the tank bottom and clamber on all fours up the bank into what was clearly an unequal situation. Their nakedness covered and mine not, their firearms in hand, the number of them as opposed to the number of me. There were possibly other areas of inequality, but I did not explore them at the time.

You came down our road, the silhouette closest to me said. *We watched you all the way.*

I thought it was a public road, I said. *I saw it on the map.*

The way we follow can't be found on any map, silhouette two informed me.

Put on your clothes, number three said.

That action was a gritty, self-conscious struggle, but I managed it. I was told to climb back through the wire, incurring another round of punctures, then to sit down in the road behind my car. My captors held the wires apart for one another, emerging puncture-free. One of them said the sheriff was on the way. That turned out to be true, but only after a very long time had passed and the sky had begun to brighten along the eastern horizon. Meanwhile, in the eerie softness of the moonlight, the three silhouettes began to have facial features. The smallest, roundest one sat cross-legged beside me, his gun across his lap. The other two alternately leaned on Judy or walked small distances along the road and back.

I realized my reportorial opportunity and tried asking questions, though I had no way of writing answers down. To break the ice, I began by offering my first name, but not my purpose. None of the three chose to offer a name in response. I let the silence settle for a while.

What does the Prophet prophesy? I finally asked the man beside me.

Water, he said.

What about water?

Lots of water.

The way he said *water* was the not the way I heard it spoken in the Moon. But it was familiar. The sound came across time and distance, from places of previous employment in cities on the eastern seaboard. Apparently the Fold was gathering from far and wide. I asked him to elaborate, but he wouldn't.

Is he major or minor? I asked. I knew very little about prophets, but had heard they could be classified as major vs. minor, like baseball players.

He's big time, the man said.

After a pause, he added *He has the Tablet of Understanding.*

He is not of the Fold, the larger man leaning on Judy above us reminded my informant, and after that he would inform no more.

Night is more reticent in the countryside than in its city cousin. There were no sirens or screeching automobiles or dance tunes in the air, just the creak of insects and, at intervals, the yip-yap of a coyote pack running far off in the distance.

We all drifted in our thoughts, dripped sweat and grew sleepy together. The man leaning on Judy asked if it would be alright for him to lie down on her back seat. I said it would, and soon the other man who had been walking on the road took over her front seat. The man beside me fell asleep with his forehead on his gun. I reclined on the gravel and joined him in unconsciousness.

The arrival of the sheriff's car woke us. I hated to leave Judy alone in that desolate spot, but there was no other choice. Chapa picked me up at the house the next day, after I was released from jail, arriving as I looked the marble in the eye. We found Judy still parked beside the Prophet's water. We saw no armed men. She started without complaint. We did run out of gas on the way home, and had to go into town for a gas can.

As we traveled, Chapa laid out his theory of *Just Afters* and *Just Befores*. Imagine, he said, that each moment has a shape. You can call it a bubble if you prefer, though of course its actual shape is shapeless. As the perpetrator of your life, you move inside that bubble, though of course it moves inside you and everywhere else. The shape comes with a kind of halo that both precedes and follows it through time. In the portion of the halo, which isn't a halo, of *Just Before*, the next moment is gathering. In the portion of *Just After*, the preceding moment dissipates. For Chapa, this explained both clairvoyance and the phenomenon of déjà vu.

Back in town, I decided to check in at the paper and update the E&P on my progress. She was not in a pleasant mood.

Where the hell is my Arledge story? She yelled as I closed her office door behind me.

I thought…

Stop thinking and bring me that story! She said, pointing at the door. The conversation was clearly over.

With all the diligence due, I sank into a period of research and produced a feature revealing that Monty's great uncle had been a deserter in World War I. It appeared that the great uncle was not a coward but a man of conscience sane enough to recognize the insanity of the war. He fled to Belgium, where he married a local woman and began a bicycle manufacturing business that still thrives today. In later years he became a noted philanthropist. A mental asylum bears his name. I thought it was an interesting story, though no doubt it reached into far deeper waters than anything I might capture on a sheet of newsprint. It ran under the headline *Family Secrets*. Before publication, the E&P edited out almost all the redeeming information on Monty's ancestor, and reworked the piece to stress instead the vile criticism he had faced at home.

Still, the E&P appeared satisfied with my work. Whether the story somehow played a healing part I don't know, but soon after it ran I

came upon her walking hand in hand with Monty down the power
tools aisle in the hardware store. The course of true love never did run
smooth.

A store employee in an orange vest gave me the Nod of Belonging.
I returned it to the best of my ability. Maybe it was the ritual of the
nod, or maybe the influence of Chapa's theories, but something moved
without moving in that moment as I observed the cloud shape of the
tall woman and the short man drift away from me, their steps in syn-
chrony. I experienced what I can only describe as one of those intuitive leaps Chapa claimed is necessary for proper cloud interpretation.
What I saw was what was missing from this particular formation: a
third figure there but not there with the two. And I knew who it was.

A brief communion with the public record told me where to find
the Arledge home. I drove there and parked Judy in front of a tall, im-
posing house set back from columns on its porch. The garden was well
tended despite the drought. Bees worked among flowers and doves
coo-coo-cooed softly in trees. From just inside the gate, I could already see the note taped to the front door. I climbed the steps to it and
read the message left there in a practiced, widely looping hand on lined
paper torn from a notebook.

Do what you will with my possessions. I have joined the Fold.
—MYRNA SAVAGE ARLEDGE

The Arledge part of the signature had been crossed out.

This is the problem with stories, the problem with closing Myrna
and Monty's gate behind me as though I knew my purpose in this life
and opening Judy's door to the sound of her by now familiar complaint—her joints ached and didn't like to be disturbed—and driving
back to the Prophet's ranch. Stories propose beginnings and middles
and endings when no such things exist. They are without exception
works of fantasy because the words to tell them live separately from

the physical substance and movements of all they attempt to describe. They leave out endless silences and vast webs of cracks that cover every surface, and almost showing through those cracks the imperceptible light of always suspected but as yet unrealized, unless in another dimension, potential for eternal falls through space. This is why one weeps. Why the eye of the beholder fails without fail to comprehend the eye of the beheld.

The sun was easing toward the west, but there was light enough to make the ranch easier to find. It still seemed a long way. I came upon a formal entrance to the property I had missed in the dark, a swinging gate over a cattle guard, with a guard house like ones you find on military bases. Inside that guard house, I recognized the smaller, rounder man who had fallen asleep on his gun beside me the night of my nude swim. He came to Judy's window.

Have you seen me before? I asked.

I've seen every inch of you, he said.

But not before that?

He looked puzzled.

My picture was in the newspaper.

We don't bother with newspapers, he said.

That's wonderful to know, I said. *I want to meet the Prophet. I want to join the Fold.*

You're right on time, he said. *He's about to give the evening talk.*

He swung open the gate.

I eased Judy onto a different surface, a smoothly paved road that ran straight between pastures with grazing, noticeably fatted cattle. Green pastures. Which struck my eye because all the other pastures in the local countryside were brown as dust. I passed a grated landing strip with a windsock and a hangar large enough to accommodate a couple of private planes, and a bulldozer parked nearby. Not much farther along I came to a turnoff onto a narrower road that led to a modest farmhouse and a series of large, new-looking outbuildings. Barns and two-story brick structures with parallel rows of windows that could have been dormitories on a campus. Off to the right I saw a sort of amphitheater where the ground had been excavated to create a lowered stage that looked up onto a sloping lawn where people had gathered and settled on blankets, waiting for something to begin. The stage was empty. There were only a couple of cars, parked under trees near the house. I left Judy there and walked to join the people on the lawn.

The men were dressed like farmhands, many in overalls. The women wore the outfits I had seen in the Moon, covered head to foot in the kind of heat and humidity where I expected shorts. All except one woman, sitting alone off to the side of the group. Her clothes might have come off the pages of *Vogue*. She was the only person in the crowd wearing sunglasses. A newcomer, I thought, and I went to sit beside her.

I wondered when you'd show up, she said, without turning her gaze from the stage.

Mrs. Arledge? I asked.

I don't care for that name, she said.

That seems a common opinion around here.

Call me Myrna if you want to call me something.

I'm sorry about the article, I said. *In the paper.*

I don't give a tinker's damn about your article, she said. She smiled. *Monty sure liked it. He got all excited and practically ran out the door.*

I'm curious why you're here, I said. *What do you know about the Prophet?*

More than most, she said.

She made me wait for an explanation. I smoothed a blade of grass and studied the beads of sweat forming at the roots of the hairs on my arm.

Who is he? I asked, when I couldn't stand any more waiting.

His name, as if it matters, is Arthur Vindman, she said. *I went to college with his sister. I made a wrong turn then, it's easy to see that now.*

I should have stayed there, not at the college, but swimming in the current of that time, and not come back here like some slave of fate to marry Monty Arledge. Even fate shouldn't be so cruel. Screw all that, though. Now I realize that's what it took to bring me where I am right now.

Arthur Vindman, she went on, was a daydream kind of person, often somewhere other than this world. His family fretted over how he might make his way. He had a job cleaning stadiums and other large venues, following events that involved crowds. Spearing Cracker Jack boxes and other detritus with a nail on the end of a stick. One bright afternoon the glint of something caught his eye, on Row 98, Section C. He poked at it with his nail and shoved it out from under the seat where it was hidden. It turned out to be a small brass tablet inscribed with what appeared to be a few words made of letters Arthur had never seen in waking life but may have encountered in his dreams. Through an act of intuitive leaping, Arthur caught the meaning of the words that instant, which was this:

Understanding and Underwater are the same.

No one other than Arthur Vindman had ever seen this Tablet. Its whereabouts were unknown and its existence was a matter of Faith. Its cryptic message formed the core of the Prophet's teachings.

Maybe he came here, of all places, Myrna said, *because I'm here. I don't care. It doesn't matter. He's here now and so am I.*

As if on cue an acolyte carried a plain, straight-backed wooden chair to the edge of the stage. All conversation ceased and all eyes focused on that spot. An unremarkable man, neither tall nor small, neither handsome nor plain, dressed in a lime green jumpsuit with a zipper up the front, walked quietly to the chair and sat down. He began speaking without prelude.

The moment of danger, he said, pausing to let the phrase hang dangerously, *is when you think you understand. Look up at the clouds.* Everyone did. The sky was the washed-out blue of midsummer, the clouds were fluffy and carefree, touched with pink and golden edges due to the angle of the sun. *Do you think the clouds are just big scoops of water vapor suspended above us in the air? Of course they are. But that is merely a fact, not a truth. In truth the clouds are messengers.* I wondered if Chapa moonlighted as a ghostwriter for the Prophet. *All over this oblivious world,* he went on, *the waters already rise and churn in a deep nostalgia. The waters know all surfaces belong to them. They were here before our trifling interference. In the depths of water, for those with eyes to see, there will be movie theaters, bedframes, tricycles, untrafficked crossroads. Above the waters, for those with ears to hear, there will be the sounds of baying hounds and church bells, coming from below. Here is the Way: Accept and welcome! Prepare within! The underwater gardens will outlive the gardeners. It will come to pass!*

The last bit was delivered with the ring of a signature Amen.

He stood and left the stage as modestly as he had come, walking toward the farm house. Apparently that was the end of the program. There were murmurs, and then the Fold began to fold its blankets and wander back to its chores. Myrna hadn't moved. I gave her the Nod of Belonging and walked away myself. When I came to Judy, I stopped and turned my face to the sky.

The clouds looked like blobs. Big blobs and lesser blobs, all on the way somewhere together.

Out of Season

Probably there is a world in which John did not get an inflatable Emily Dickinson for Christmas.

But in this world, in Sister Pauline's living room, the package Emily came wrapped in could have held a fluffy robe. John was put off, but didn't think it showed. He laughed as best he could with everybody else, the adults anyway—the kids were off with their new gadgets—from his seat in Dad's old chair, right beside the tree. Through the window behind him the light worked toward brightness for the first time in days, the grayness peeling away. A pool of cold sunlight formed on the floor.

The gift came with an undercurrent, he knew. It said things. The inspiration could only have come from Little Mikey, the b'n-law himself, though Sister Pauline would have giggled at the idea. Where on Earth did they find it? The tag on the package said *From the Family* ♥ .

How did you know? he asked the room, in a voice that peaked and squeaked a little for effect. *I've been looking everywhere for one of these!* This got another laugh. Little Mikey led a chant of *Blow her up! Blow her up!* but John didn't open the box, and when the laughter drizzled out attentions turned to the next person holding a present. One-at-a-time openings, so that everyone could comment as the present was revealed, were a central rhythm of holiday tradition reaching back at least as far as John and Sister Pauline's parents. Dad would watch from this same chair, the one he called Traveler because he settled in it afternoons to nap and dream.

The gifting done, John waited for his opportunity and took his leave before the post-feast-and-gaiety torpor settled in. No one protested. To leave a place is to vanish.

Driving home, he felt a composed anxiety. He was well within himself, able to examine things. He must have told someone—in a vulnerable moment—that Emily was his secret heartthrob. He would not have said obsession. He would not have revealed that when he visited Emily's home in Amherst he had dared to run his hand along the footboard of her bed, that he kept a photo of her gravestone archived on a backup drive and a copy of her portrait as a teenager framed on the wall of his study, with the door to that room closed when visitors were in the house. Lacking those details, the admission would have sounded innocent enough, not simple to weaponize. He would never have confessed to Sister Pauline and God knows not Little Mikey. Someone put the bug in Mikey's ear. It could only have been Laurel, Sister Pauline's bff since childhood, the one woman in their crowd he had daydreamed over in his youth, and if he was honest, often since. Her face appeared before him now, thickened from its girlish shape, with its wedgey, curious nose, small eyes, and Cupid's bow lips, inviting disclosure. Laurel! Of all the people to confide in. He felt sure she and Little Mikey were having an affair. Little Mikey had confidence with women, impossible to say why. Did Laurel laugh with all the others when he opened the package? Of course she did. She sat by Little Mikey on the couch and they laughed together, while Sister Pauline watched them from the opposite side of the room. In a weird way, though, the whole thing was an affirmation. Didn't Emily experience her own betrayals, suffer through her own family issues? This just gave them more to hold in common.

He had chosen his gifts for others well, he believed. He only gave books—real books, not E-books—whether the recipient was a known reader or not, and he made a game of connecting the books to the interests of their readers, imagining interests when he didn't know them. There was hardly any traffic. Outside his car, the brief gift of light began its escape from the world. Unordered shipments of mundane thoughts arrived at his mental doorstep, along with a few mediocre ideas. What did he need from the grocery? Was it even open? What if everybody felt a vibration like a buzzing phone every time they made a bad decision? *Brrrrrt. Don't unlock your little vault of secrets for Laurel.*

Toby greeted him at the door, 143 pounds of Newfoundland. Yes, Emily had a Newfoundland too, but he was Carlo, after the dog in *Jane Eyre. You ask of my companions,* she wrote to Thomas Wentworth Higginson. *Hills, sir, and the sundown, and a dog as large as myself that my father bought me. They are better than human beings, because they know but do not tell.* He let Toby out in the yard, carried the Emily box inside along with his other gifts—he could rely on the Christmas party for a shirt or sweater, at least one pair of socks, various gift cards in small denominations, and treats and toys for Toby—cleared a space on the coffee table and set everything down. The stack looked comfortable there so he left it in place for a couple of weeks. One day as he passed, for no particular reason, he hung the shirt in the closet and put the socks in the drawer. He stuck the hoodie with the Lakers logo—another gag gift, everyone knew he was a Spurs fan—in the Lawn'n Leaf bag he kept for donation runs to Goodwill. He picked up Emily's box and added it to the bag, paced around the room twice and took it back out. *Why?* His house was cluttered with objects he rarely touched or admired, and this one meant nothing more than a backhanded insult, more to Emily than to him. Maybe he thought he'd set the box upright somewhere as an ironic acknowledgement of a culture gone wrong. But that was unlikely. He did not welcome irony. The world was coated with it, like a layer of thin ice.

He sorted that day's mail and opened the hand crafted thank-you card from his favorite niece, Stephie, who was eight.

Dear Uncle John,
Thank you for The Secret Garden. It is sad. Daddy asked Mommy if she thought you were sleeping with Emily. Who is Emily?

He moved the box, without a look inside, to the top of a bookcase and covered it with two stacks of literary magazines.

Emily waited there in the womb of her box for a good six months. Meanwhile John left each weekday morning for his job at the state Capitol, on the staff of the Sunset Advisory Commission, where he aggregated data and compiled reports on the malfunctions of state bureaucracies. The job was not demanding. His role, as he understood it, was to justify the Commission's existence, and his own salary, by recommending the elimination of as many state agencies as possible. The purpose of his recommendations, apparently, was to stimulate the lobbyists who profited from representing clients before the agencies in question to make contributions to the politicians on the Commission, who then ignored John's work product.

He returned home each evening around 6:30 depending on traffic, and spent his nights reading and his weekends gardening—during her lifetime, Emily was better known as a gardener than a poet. He took Toby on outings, went to a couple of basketball games and a couple of birthday parties for nieces and nephews. The gift burrowed to the bottom of his consciousness.

In July he took a week of his vacation time. He had no plans, just time on his hands. One morning as he shuffled through the magazines on the bookcase the forgotten box materialized in his field of vision like the ghost of Christmas past.

The box was easy to ignore. It lacked any attempt at design. Why didn't it show the arresting daguerreotype of the teenaged Emily, the one that hung a few steps away in his study, with her hair parted in the center and pulled severely down and back across her ears, the adornment of velvety ribbon secured around a graceful neck with a pin that catches the light, the countenance that says don't look away but look from where you are? The box only offered the words INFLATABLE IMMORTALS in thick black type, a bubbly logo that said Happy Family, a disclaimer-size notation that said Made in China, and Emily's name on an adhesive label as an afterthought, so small you could miss it if you didn't want to know which immortal lived inside.

There could be no harm in having a look.

He snapped the tape from the sides of the box and pulled off the top. Good Lord. There was the face from the portrait, monstrously twisted. The folded body off-gassed with a delicate toxicity. John lifted the deflated Emily gently from her confines and settled her on the table. He retrieved his air compressor from the utility room. Was he really doing this? Apparently. If the thing was as ridiculous as it promised to be, he could always squeeze the air back out of it, fold it up as best he could and stick it in the Goodwill bag.

John had just read a book celebrating the human lung. *Independent life begins the instant that the lungs inflate.* He spread the body on the floor, flattening its creases. It wore a plastic imprint of the famous white dress of cotton piqué. What a mistake! With five minutes of research the Happy Family people could have learned that the face of the portrait and the dress came from two vastly different periods. John inserted the needle he used to pump up balls into a valve in Emily's low back. The air compressor made a chugging racket. Toby lumbered in to check it out, then paced around her barking as she came into being in front of him, her folds gradually parting as her form arose and her features beginning to emerge. Her nacreous skin might have squeaked had John run his hands over it, which he wouldn't do. Her eyes had a luster that could not be attributed to the lighting in the room. Without evidence, her makers had given her a pair of lace-up ankle boots. They did get her height about right, John thought. He had been part of an online discussion group that settled on Emily's height at five foot three via the dimensions of her coffin. *I am small,* she wrote to Higginson, *like the wren, and my hair is bold, like the chestnut bur, and my eyes like the sherry in the glass that the guest leaves.* The surface representing hair on plastic Emily was more like dried blood, the eyes more luminant pancake than sherry.

The thing taking form before him was wrong as could be, a cruel parody of Emily, but he couldn't bring himself to deflate it and send it away. On an impulse he finished off the last few smoothing bits with his own breath, his lips fixed on the valve as he knelt beside her on the floor. When he set her upright she bounced a little on her heels. He stepped back to view her from across the small room, and Toby joined him. He expected disappointment and regret. Instead he witnessed a presence. All the objects he kept and periodically admired had a desperate, clinging quality, begging not to be ignored. This one was different. At first sight it announced itself as a being with its own rights in his home—a resident and not a visitor—independent, self-possessed, peacefully demanding. Also, and more unsettling, as an avatar of an unknowable field of possibility. After Higginson visited Emily in Amherst for the first and only time, in 1870, he wrote that he had never been near *anyone who drained my nerve power so much. Without touching her, she drew from me. I am glad not to live near her.*

Emily's emergence there before him brought John the gift of the same very particular, and very particularly nameless, discomfort. He considered and judged as inadequate or inane a series of statements and questions. He stood and gaped. Emily looked back with an inexpressible expression. Not blank. Not indifferent. Engaged but more with distance than with John. Toby was less intimidated. He danced heavily around the floor, making the whinish sound that meant he wanted to play. No one really knows why the original Emily became so committed a recluse—as if she needed a reason. Some think the final straw came when her only constant companion, her dog Carlo, died. The first to greet her when she went to heaven, she told a neighbor child, would be *this dear, faithful old friend*. Toby padded to Emily and nudged her at the knees. She tipped forward with a charming delicacy so that her inflated fingers touched the crown of Toby's broad head. Had she moved through her own agency, or was Toby the sole cause of the effect?

Without question, Toby's enthusiasm broke the ice, and allowed John a moment of cognitive success. *Welcome*, he said, earnestly. For a long moment, he and Emily regarded one another. It then occurred to him that the hospitable thing would be to introduce her to her new surroundings. He lifted her gently and carried her through all the rooms of his small home, with a slow perusal of the bookcases. He stooped and held her horizontally to view the lower shelves, but it seemed too odd to turn her upside down so she could see the volumes on the lowest. Toby trailed along, tossing out occasional happy barks. Only a few of these books, John realized, would be familiar, but he felt no need to narrate. He imagined Emily might be impressed by the sheer accumulation of the pages, but she kept any thoughts to herself. The silence settled between them and stayed.

Naturally John stopped with her face pointed toward the spines of her own books. *The Collected Poems*, *The Selected Poems*, *The Letters*, and his most recent acquisition, *The Gorgeous Nothings*, with its reproductions of Emily's penciled words on random scraps of paper, mostly torn from envelopes. *Oh wait*, he thought, *I've got something that she has to see*. Knowing she would understand, he set Emily down carefully and went to the cabinet where he kept the lovingly wrapped and boxed 1890 first edition of *Poems First Series* that had cost him three months' salary. He showed her the cover with its Ghost Flowers painting and then, with all due reverence, opened the book to "Because I Could Not Stop for Death," and held Emily face down so she could take it in. *Poems First Series* was published four years after Emily died. She saw it for the first time now, in John's house. The book beneath Emily's face was edited by Higginson and Mabel Loomis Todd, who painted the Ghost Flowers to assert herself onto the very front of the volume, and who was involved in a long, scandalous affair with Emily's brother Austin at the time. What might she make of it? Higginson and Todd had altered the text to their own liking, even added titles, which Emily disdained. How much did she know of the tangled web of family dysfunction that surrounded the book—the battles over literary rights, the land disputes and lawsuits?

Austin Dickinson lived next door to Emily with his wife Susan. Some people who knew no better thought Emily herself had an affair with Susan, her sometimes best friend and first reader. John dismissed these fantasies for what they were. He was certain Emily never indulged in anything beyond emotional affairs with anyone. When Emily's brother took his lover Mabel to play piano and sing for his mother and his sisters, Emily listened from the shadows in the hall. Afterwards Mabel wrote that people in Amherst called Emily *the myth. She has not been out of her house for fifteen years…she seems to be the climax of all the family oddity.* John turned a few more pages and gave Emily time with each poem. How strange it must have been for her to encounter her own words, not scratched on envelopes but printed on a page! He set her upright to recover her bearings and allowed a respectful period for reflection.

Meanwhile, John wondered which room Emily would like for her own. He knew she needed her own space, but as far as he could tell, she expressed no preference. There was only one bedroom. The study—which served as his home office—made the best sense, he decided. It had the most books, a desk, good lamps, and a comfortable chair.

He left Emily to settle in and spent the balance of the afternoon arranging a small computer station for himself in a corner of his bedroom and moving the necessary home office files. Toby fell asleep at Emily's feet. The hardwood floor in the study looked uncomfortable,

so John placed Emily on a small wool rug and moved Toby's sleeping
platform and its memory foam mattress in from the bedroom.

While John worked, he did not worry about Emily. He knew she
was adjusting to her reincarnation with an enviable grace. She had
traveled from nowhere to arrive in an encasement of plastic skin. She
would bear this philosophically. Being nobody was a comfort zone for
her. She could not deny having always been disgracefully self-centered,
so in this particular afterlife it was meet that she be so contained. She
was selfless now, but present. She needed little news. Through plain
osmosis she would understand enough to puzzle out a world of squalid
imaginings and discarded pasts. She would feel at home.

The routine of the amended household was soon established. John
knocked discreetly on Emily's door each morning, and looked in on
her. If she had lost a breath of air and acquired a wrinkle in the night,
he donated his own breath to her valve until she smoothed again. He
let Toby out in the yard, prepared his breakfast, and took Emily a
steaming offering of tea in a china cup ornamented with larkspur. He
thought she might enjoy the aroma. Often he carried her out to a spot
beside the dining nook, for the company. He was tempted to speak to
her of current events or things he was reading, and even more so to
indulge in the presumption of discussing her work or her life. Instead
he chose to honor their silent bond. Who knew which topics were
most tender? After feeding Toby and tidying up, he returned her to her
room with books of contemporary poetry—what would she think of
them?—stacked with some Emily and some Wordsworth and Brown-
ing, for the familiarity, on the fair copy of her Amherst writing desk
he bought to place in front of her, with the room door open so Toby
could come and go.

When John wasn't thinking about her during his workday, he felt
he should be. Back home, he took Toby for his walk and brought Emily in to join him at dinner. The evenings were still too hot to sit outside, so he read with her in the study for half an hour before leaving

her to her privacy. One Saturday morning before the heat could climb, Emily stood in the shade while John broke ground for the fall garden.

That night, John dreamed. Turning the soil for the garden, he uncovered a hole. He understood that the hole was the entrance to a narrow tunnel, searched for an exit but couldn't find one, then realized that the tunnel looped underneath the property and from there below the dermis of the entire planet, beneath oceans and the churning organisms of cities. As he peered into the entrance he heard the pumping of machinery below, the metal heartbeats of a mine. Toby appeared and sniffed at the hole. He picked up the scent of an animal somewhere below, and before John could stop him he dove in. The tunnel was just wide enough for Toby to descend, but not enough for him to turn around. John reached in to try to grab the dog's back legs, but he was gone. John called and whistled. He was afraid to dig into the tunnel because it might collapse on Toby. He considered drilling air shafts but didn't know where to dig and didn't have the proper tools. John paced, in a panic. He knew Toby's time was running out. He cried out and woke himself up. Then he screamed because Emily stood over him in the darkness at the side of the bed. She had come from her room to comfort him. Emily was luminous. Her white dress gleamed. The darkness had entered her and come back out as light. Toby stood happily beside her. The waves of his breath rolled onto John's face.

Had she floated over? John wondered. *Had she bounced?*

It took John a long time to fall asleep again. When he did, Emily drifted to the window by his bed, a better window than the one in her room because it looked out on the city from a small hill. Within the light cast by its electric power, the city struggled to believe in itself.

In the morning he found her staring at the bathroom mirror.

They began to sit together through the evenings, or she stood in her way, in her containment, and he sat not at her side but within the same togetherness. They each had their memories. When outdoors, John no longer waved to neighbors but instead faced inward, toward Emily and their abode. She might be framed in the screen door, within the grid it made of the world. The house that sheltered them maintained a share in the neighborhood's perch upon a temporal reality, but progressed steadily toward a separate existence as an unaffiliated craft adrift in spacetime. Perhaps all habitations are the same.

John declined an invitation to a backyard barbeque in celebration of the 15th Anniversary of Sister Pauline's and Little Mikey's marriage, pleading nonexistent work demands. In fact he had arranged to work from home. His fellow staffers at Sunset Advisory did not perceive a difference between his physical presence and his virtual absence. He left home only for necessities. He had no interest in being elsewhere.

You've never missed our anniversary, Sister Pauline said into the phone, in the higher register her voice attained when she was agitated.

Try to stay married and I'll catch you next year, John said. He didn't necessarily believe it.

Time moved rapidly outside the house and slowly inside. Outside, the seasons did not wish to give up turning. John fed the birds who arrived to spend the winter, from bags of seed he bought online. He left out dishes of sugar water and fruit for the bees. As he worked at these tasks he was tormented by his autumn allergies. He chuffled, sneezed, and coughed, filled his pockets with tissues. His ailments did not keep him from the garden. Emily suffered no afflictions. He knew she was eager to see the planting done. While she stood over him, a witness, he laid out a tray of heliotropes because her sister-in-law Susan had placed those flowers in Emily's hand as she lay in her casket. As he dug into the mysterious soil, stopping now and then to wipe the drops that ran from his nose, sunlight and those other—imperceptible!—rays that strike the Earth from space cascaded down. Who can comprehend the grand web of connection, the restless confluence that transformed the rock he turned up in the trowel into a speckled egg?

An anxious thought came from above him and he froze. True, the water nymph Clytie, according to Ovid, transubstantiated into a heliotrope when she was betrayed by Helios, the sun god, and now turned forever in flowery form to follow the path of the sun. But heliotropes would never do. Didn't he know they could be toxic to dogs?

The Re-Make

There are twelve days of Christmas and twenty-nine or thirty days of Ramadan, depending on the moon. Passover lasts seven or eight days, depending on the custom of your ancestors. These phenomena may be limited in scope, but they endure. Most do not. For example, the video store.

Once almost as essential as a phone jammed with apps, the video store lived an unassuming life in an ancient time. Now it exists among the ghosts. People have reported coming upon video stores at random intersections, bustling with customers and palpable as Quaker Oats, only to watch them dematerialize into the world behind this one. These visions are ubiquitous as the World War II soldier, fully uniformed and drinking coffee at a kitchen table, who appears to the insomniac as she glides listlessly to her refrigerator for a glass of milk, then vanishes as she glances away without registering what she has seen until the morning.

Many of the stores were chain operations subject to a corporate hierarchy. Others were of the Mom and Pop variety, not dressed in a standardized façade or decorated in accord with a graphic standards manual from a marketing department. The difference between the corporate store and the M&P, if it need be explained (and it may, with both entities living only in the past) is that chain stores are bereft and soulless—it is not their fault, it is just the way things are—and each M&P is soulfully alive and thus, like all souled things, owns a story at once necessary and impossible to tell. For example, the story of the Big Show Video stores now materializing before you on the page, where Pop is Ronnie Cromwell and Mom once had been, would have been, Ronnie's not late but latest wife Verna, had she not filed, in some bitterness, for divorce in recent times. With three locations serving different neighborhoods, Big Show represents the apex of Ronnie's career as a self-taught, hard knocks entrepreneur. Stock boy in a grocery. Pan scrubber in a pizzeria. Deck swabber in the Navy. No paperwad degree and no silver spoon. Clawed his way up into management at a sporting goods chain, but chafed in the harness of an employee. Ronnie had ideas. He needed room to make his moves. He knew the next big thing. He began with a fishkeeping store, selling Tetras, Oscars, Mollies, Cherry Barbs, baby Red-Eared Slider turtles, aquaria and supplies. But a fungus killed much of his stock and the business ran dry. He then put all he had, and all the bank would spare, into retail video. If ever there was a sure thing, he thought. He saw it! Everybody loves the movies. Who wouldn't want to take their favorite movies home—on tape!—to watch and rewind and watch again anytime they liked? His admirers, and no small number of his detractors, of whom there is a Tabernacle choir, know him as Ronnie Movie.

In terms of the physical dimension, Big Show stores have in common the fact that they are rectangles of cinder block construction, divided about two-thirds of the way down the long side by a wall to separate the store's two primary trade activities. The front section deals in family movies, cartoons, comedies, dramas, and adventures, with small sub-sections dedicated to documentaries, classics, and foreign films. The back section, less brightly lit, deals in porn. The sections have their own entrances at the front and rear of the building, respectively, their own cash registers and dedicated personnel.

As a natural promoter, Ronnie offers the occasional special event in each of the Big Shows, attuned to the interests of the front door or back door customers. He is particularly though anxiously pleased about the back door event he has scheduled for today. A porn actress of legend will make an in-person appearance in each of the stores. For reasons Ronnie does not wish to consider because he already considers them his every waking moment, today's promotion is critical. He has invested in three life-size cardboard representations of the celebrity and painted posters announcing her visit with his own hands. She is past due and his nerves are on edge.

As Ronnie stands at the counter in front Big Show exchanging factoids on *The Sound of Music* with the pale, nervous regular whose only adventure outside his home is his weekly trip to Big Show, a noticeably large man in a muscle shirt swings open the glass door at the entrance and holds it to admit a nun in a floor length black habit. The Sister's hands are clasped in front of her as if in prayer. Her eyes are striking, even at a distance. She takes in the store. It looks back at her like a cave looks back at an oracle. It is as if they knew each other long ago and now struggle to locate that forgotten knowledge in a particular time and place.

I'll be damned, Ronnie says, frightening the pale man. Ronnie feels foolish—of course!—how could he forget her biggest seller, *Ten Hale Marys,* still renting like hotcakes after its release in the early days of video cassettes?

The actress has ignored a specific request to enter through the back door. Ronnie leaves the pale man and greets her with a quick handshake and a million dollar smile. He escorts her briskly through a sparse weekend crowd that consists of one distracted mom, her hide and seeking children, two pimply, bewildered teenagers, and one omnipresent film geek, to and through the door that separates front Big Show from back Big Show. The muscle-shirted man follows closely. The walls of the store watch the trio pass and record the memory.

The small group of customers waiting in back Big Show turn and appraise the new arrivals carefully. There is light, confused applause.

Very efficient design, muscle shirt man remarks. *I'll wager you make a buck.*

I've still got the first one, Ronnie says.

Handler, the large man says, and nods in a not unfriendly way.

I'm Ronnie, Ronnie says.

It's not a name, it's a function, the man says. *I'm the Handler.* Extending down the front of the muscle shirt, the Handler wears a long gold chain supporting a pendant with XOXO spelled out in four inch high gold letters. There are diamonds on the serifs of the X's. The tummy inside the shirt extends outward just enough that the pendant's message angles upward for a more comfortable reading experience. The Handler is a hirsute man.

I'm grateful to Henry for putting this together, Ronnie says.

Not Henry, the Handler says. *A new guy.*

What happened to Henry? Ronnie wants to know. Henry has been Ronnie's distributor for the back door side of the business since he first got started. A trusted soul.

Suicide, the Handler says. *A tragic business. He put his feet in a tub of cement, waited 'til it dried, drug himself to the George Washington Bridge and flung himself over, tub first. He was wearing nice shoes at the time, Armanis, which he did not bother to remove.*

They used to bury suicides at the crossroads, the Sister says so quietly Ronnie has to lean toward her to understand. *When the coroner's verdict was felo de se, they drove a stake through your heart and buried you without benefit of exequy. Perhaps the crossroad was a kind of consolation prize. At least you got planted near a cross. Some historians speculate that crossroads were simply the place to go, because that's where they hung criminals. And then there's the theory that the crossroad would confuse the ghost. I don't know how much demand there might be for confused ghosts. The practice pretty much stopped after Lord Castlereagh slit his own throat in 1822. Of course he was one of the elite, we wouldn't know about him if he wasn't. Quite the career. He had put down the Irish rebellion and recruited the coalition that defeated Napoleon and used the Royal Navy to stop the slave trade, but an old case of syphilis caught up with him and twisted him paranoid in a radical way. Due to his high standing, Britannia waved the rules and buried him in Westminster Abbey. Not everybody was on board, though. He wasn't universally admired. Lord Bryon penned a ditty suggesting that people should piss on his grave. In Westminster Abbey. Imagine.*

The world does not distinguish among follies, the Handler says. *It has not the means.*

She certainly knows her history, Ronnie says.

You might address your comments directly to the Sister, the Handler says, a little testily. *She's standing right here.*

Ronnie is a bit intimidated, he has to admit. Here is a famous personage, the flesh and blood manifestation of the distinctly more unclothed cardboard cutout the Sister stands beside. Together with her presence there is the amazement of the faultlessly modest demeanor, the downcast eyes, the actor thoroughly absorbed into her role. Ronnie turns to the Sister to deliver his compliment, but stops in his tracks. If he simply repeats what he has said to the Handler, he realizes, the remark could be interpreted as patronizing. Of course the Sister knows her history, and why should she not? And on what grounds might he assume the contrary, or be surprised in any way at such knowledge? Does the implication of such surprise amount to an assumption that a woman in her profession knows little of such matters? Why would he believe so? Is he so ruled by prejudice and chauvinism as to be blind to the possibilities that surround him? The human depths he blithely ignores? And at the end of the day what does he himself know about crossroads burials or any other matter, that might place him in a superior position?

Awkwardly, Ronnie performs a kind of stilted bow meant to signify an honorific offering before the Sister, whose eyes remain downcast throughout, and says nothing.

He then steps away and invites the assembled customers in back Big Show to form a line if they aspire to chat with the Sister and perhaps receive an autograph. More customers are drifting in. The door from front Big Show opens and in come the distracted mom and her restless brood of little ones.

We thought she might be the Flying Nun, the mom says. *But she doesn't have the cornette with little wings. Is what she has called a cornette or a veil?*

Can she fly? A red headed child in pig tails wants to know.

Can you? A smaller and differently sexed version of the same child asks the Sister, grasping her index finger.

The Sister smiles benevolently, without showing teeth. *The question is not whether I can fly,* she says, *but whether I wish to fly. It's a matter of controversy. St. Joseph of Cupertino, who was born in 1603, was always flying around the chapel, and various other places, in ecstasies of adoration. His superiors were always ordering him to come down because the parishioners were watching him fly instead of keeping their heads bowed. He wasn't particularly bright. As a child his teachers thought of him as cognitively impaired. People said since God made the world with physical laws that didn't include flying humans, a person in flight amounted to an act of defiance against God. They thought the flying business was just a spiritual stunt. A curious thing about St. Joseph is that when he was celebrating mass he might get all filled with the spirit and float up to the ceiling and stay there for hours, and when he came down he would take up the mass in the same place he left off.*

She's not the stupid Flying Nun, a third, verge of teenage child in a ball cap says. *Let's go back to the cartoons.*

The event is a success. Ronnie is pleased. There is perhaps three times the usual traffic for a Saturday afternoon in back Big Show. But there is also an increasing problem. Because of the Sister's late arrival, the events at the other two Big Show stores are in danger of becoming non-events, with disappointed customers and a star that never shows and shines. A very bad thing. Ronnie has carefully appointed the kick-off times for each event to allow for an hour in the first store, travel time, an hour in the second store, and so on. Only ten minutes remain of the hour scheduled for the first store, and customers are still arriving. Ronnie exits by the back door and paces 'round the building, three times, four times, in a high state of distress. The building, an empathic structure, feels him. What will he do? He has estimated travel time from store one to store two at twenty to twenty-five minutes, given lighter weekend traffic. He has allowed an additional five minutes travel time to be on the safe side. Further delay here could push the entire schedule, not to mention the entire enterprise, over the metaphoric cliff.

He re-enters back Big Show, intending to move things along. The line to visit with the Sister has grown longer. It stretches almost to the door. He observes that the line is not moving. To investigate, he takes a position near the Sister. The fan in front of her, an older man with thinning hair, glasses with thick black frames and a worn tweed sports coat, is on his knees.

How long has it been since your last confession? The Sister whispers.

A nun can't hear confession! Ronnie pleads to the Handler.

The Lord works in mysterious ways, the Handler replies.

I'm not a Catholic, the man on his knees whispers back.

Tell me anyway, the Sister says. There is intimacy, urgency in the demand.

I didn't call my mother for a year, the penitent says. *I was afraid of her. Then she died.*

You stinker, the Sister says. *You're lucky I didn't bring my dominatrix gear.* She chucks the man's chin playfully. *Do you have any idea what that woman went through to bring you into the world?*

I'm truly sorry, the man says. *And I humbly repent.*

Repentance requires action, the Sister replies. *Find an old lady and do chores around her house. Now go in peace.*

The man rises and gratefully departs. The next man kneels.

We really need to speed this up, Ronnie tells the Handler, regretting the whining tone that has crept into his voice.

The "this" you want to rush is called bonding with the fans, the Handler says, dismissing him. *It's a pearl of great price, and they will remember it forever. They will share it with their grandchildren. There is no substitute.*

The confessions grind on. Ronnie dances back through the door to check on front Big Show, where one of his two last remaining employees at this location, a twenty-something slacker named Justin whose one redeeming virtue is his detailed knowledge of every movie ever made, relaxes on a stool behind the counter, watching Jimmy Stewart's nightmare scene in *Vertigo* on the wall-mounted monitor. The sound is turned off. The pale, nervous man stands at the counter talking to the back of Justin's head about *The Sound of Music.*

Isn't it a lucky turn when the abbess sees that Julie Andrews is unfit to be a postulant, and sends her to the villa to be the children's governess? The pale, nervous man is saying.

Maria is the postulant, Justin says to Jimmy Stewart, who is walking toward an open grave. *Julie Andrews is the actor. Maria is the character.*

On the screen, psychedelic rays stream from Jimmy Stewart's head.

Julie Andrews was Eliza Doolittle and Queen Guinevere and Cinderella and Mary Poppins, the pale, nervous man says. *She was born out of wedlock.*

Justin nods.

But fate is so uncanny, the pale, nervous man says. *Too numinous for anyone to read it. The way Julie and Christopher Plummer get together goes beyond unexpected. No one could have seen it coming. And the escape from the Nazis! Remember, Christopher Plummer, as a retired Naval officer, would have been forced to serve in the German navy if it weren't for the abbess. Plus, Paramount had the rights to the story to begin with. If they had made the picture, Audrey Hepburn would have been Maria.*

Ronnie pours himself an overcooked cup of coffee from the percolator, tries to dump in powdered creamer but only gets dust from the empty container. Rejects the coffee. Exits at the front and paces in the parking lot, seeing nothing that he sees, hearing the same. The morning had been cool. The afternoon sizzles. Re-enters back Big Show. The line for confession is as long as before, perhaps longer. Standing by the Sister, he notes that her patience grows thin with her flock. Her responses are becoming blunt, even insensitive.

Reacting to a sudden, overwhelming need, Ronnie steps in line ahead of the next man up.

My turn, fucker, the man says. *I've been waiting for an hour.*

It's my store, Ronnie says, and falls to his knees facing the pleated black curtain of the Sister's tunic.

Okay, baby boy, what's your big problem? The Sister asks impatiently.

I am not what I seem, Ronnie says. *My life is no longer a coherent whole. I have made unfortunate decisions.*

Join the club, she says. *You're absolved or reconciled or whatever, so move on.*

As the confessions continue for another full hour, Ronnie places calls to Big Show 2 and Big Show 3, instructing the employee in each store to inform the customers waiting in the back of the delay, and reschedule the appearance and autograph signing for later in the day. Possibly in the evening.

What time should I tell them? Sky, the junior college dropout in charge at Big Show 3, wants to know.

I wish I knew, Ronnie says. *Maybe four hours from now. Maybe five. Thank them for their patience. Suggest that they do something productive in the meantime, and return. Ask your Mom to get some chips and dips and soda from the Quickie Pickie, and put them out in back. Tell her I'll reimburse. And,* he thinks to add, *call Weasel at number 2 and have him call his Mom and do the same.*

Weasel isn't talking to his Mom, the phone receiver says.

Then tell him to call anybody he is still talking to, Ronnie says.

Staggering, that's the word. If he isn't staggering he should be. The world is too much with him. Sleep no longer comforts him in its strange balm. It visits only as a rude guest, and the dreams it brings are eschatological. His eyes burn like marbles left unattended near a flame. All the travails of the small businessman are his, plus a few. He has expanded too fast, exceeding his means and his cash flow. His lease payments and accounts payable are late and getting later. They approach the witching hour. The banks treat his loan applications like they are radioactive. His few remaining reserves are subject to the court's judgment. Verna's lawyer is a boundless asshole, working overtime to consume him alive, shit him out and flush him down. In what he now realizes is a surpassingly bad and possibly terminal move, he has resorted to a line of credit at bloodsucking rates arranged through Henry, his contact at the porn distributor, now sleeping with the fishes. And worst of all for his long-term prospects, should there be a long term in his future, the world that is too much with him is rapidly leaving him behind. Cable TeeVee is everywhere, even in the desolate apartment he rents in his exile by divorce, its channels constantly expanding, its content offerings as accessible as a flip of a remote. Grocery stores are installing video kiosks for instant gratification. New technology makes movies new and old, smutty and squeaky clean, ever easier to access. Some doom prophets even predict the day will come when a consumer can order up any movie she desires, instantly, from the comfort of her couch. Clearly, the

Grim Reaper owns the mortgage on the industry segment Ronnie has chosen as his lifeline.

At long last the Sister emerges from the back room, accompanied by the Handler.

I need a drink, she says.

I'm sorry, but we really don't have time, Ronnie replies.

She gives him a look that casts him to the Ninth Circle of Hell. The Handler's accompanying look confirms that free will is no longer an option. They enter Ronnie's Ford Fairlane, the Sister in front and the Handler in the rear, and head toward a fern bar ten blocks away, in the opposite direction from Big Show 2. The building is sad to see them go. At first, traffic is unexpectedly heavy. Then traffic may not be called traffic at all, because traffic implies motion and this phenomenon, seeking a new name, does not move. It does not inch. It does not exist, except as an idea. There must be an accident ahead, or road construction or a nuclear explosion. The carjam is constructed of the behemoths of the era, frantically polluting as they block all progress in a fit of noncooperation with one another.

Ronnie studies his watch like a small table of cryptograms, for a new answer. But the answer is always the same. Not a single starry-eyed soul will be waiting at the next store, or the next after that, for the promised visit of the movie star who never, ever arrives. No one has such patience, such love and strength of character anymore. The promotion is doomed, he concludes. It cannot be counted as more than a one-third success, and even that calculation fails to take into account the incalculable cost of alienation as applied to customers of Big Show 2 and Big Show 3. Customers so broken-hearted they may be lost forever. There are other video stores. There are TeeVees and kiosks and titty bars. When was this sour destiny of his first set in motion? In the heavens on the day he was born? The moment he was conceived? His father Arthur pumping home the false-hearted, engendering sperm into his mother Alma Lee, an image he has never dared imagine and cannot now admit? Is it too much to ask, a negligible measure of success in a treacherous world? For Ronnie, the measure would not come through love, that much is clear. Before Verna, two other women, people of good quality themselves but poor ingredients when stirred into a cocktail that included himself, had stood with him at church door. He did not deny his own faults. For one, he had never understood monogamy as a synonym of forever. But business stands outside such understandings. Business is his refuge, his métier, his first and last mirage.

This model is subject to various problems in reliability, the Sister says, as they practice the discipline of immobility together in the beige sedan. *The accessory belt tensioner requires frequent replacement. Should it fail, the accessory belt itself may snap, endangering in their turns the power steering, alternator, and water pump. It is entirely possible that they all go kaput. I note a rattling noise at idle, possibly due to a loose exhaust heat shield.*

I know one thing, the Handler says. *This tour is encouraging to say the least. Clearly a situation of pent-up demand. People live in anticipation of new content. And with improvements in format compatibility, portability, improved camera tubes and circuitry, editing functionality, and radically better picture resolution, not even to mention the mother lodes that are the new avenues of distribution that go so far beyond the brick and mortar video outlets, the coming industry will surpass the old in every way. A true sense of excitement is brewing in the organization.*

What do you have in mind? Ronnie inquires. He hates himself in desperate ways for every plan he has ever made, every thought his overheated brain has generated, every dream he has borrowed from the grand library of dreams only to squander.

For starters, a re-make of Ten Hale Marys, and thus the inhabited appearance of our star in this very vehicle. Together with other titles from that era.

That is exciting, Ronnie says. He wonders about Henry, the release he must have felt in his long plunge from the bridge. Did he fall at the same rate he would have without a tub of cement around his ankles, or at a faster clip?

A godsend for your business, possibly, the Handler says. *Depending. But most definitely for ours.*

Through the insufficient air conditioning inside the car, through the rolled-up window past the Sister's steadfast profile, Ronnie watches pedestrians flow smoothly on a sidewalk, performing amazing acts of speed relative to he himself as the driver of a V-8 powered internal combustion machine that represents the epitome, the ultimate result, of man's relationship with fire. The car ahead moves half a car-length, and Ronnie takes his foot off the brake to creep forward. There is an unpleasant scent of steaming water as produced in the company of rubber and various metals. A cloud begins to seep from the seams of the car's long hood, taking shape before Ronnie's inadequately lubricated eyes like the mist that would obscure the appearance of a wizard in an ancient myth.

Water pump, the Sister says. *I'm going to pray that we make it to the bar.*

Without a moment's hesitation, the jam begins to break. Cars ahead are moving as if they never thought of standing still. Ronnie pushes on. The steam cloud boils over and dispenses around them as they go, as though they are on fire. All the traffic lights turn green. The road is darker than it should be. In the distance they have left behind, the building worries over them.

Ronnie turns into the fern bar parking lot and the trinity leaves the Fairlane smoking in place.

The soul of the fern bar is confused. Perhaps it is not what it seems. Perhaps its life is not a coherent whole, and it has made unfortunate decisions. Singles sit across from one another beneath fake Tiffany lamps, sipping sugary drinks and generating all they have of charm. Carrot sticks, celery sticks, broccoli and cauliflower florets, mixed nuts and tublets of Ranch dressing await at the buffet. Captain & Tennille sing *Love Will Keep Us Together* on the sound system, at a volume omnipresent but not too loud and not too soft. The fronds of ferns extend from planters, listening indifferently. Ronnie first met Verna at a not so different place, with other lamps and other music and other plants listening. They laughed and laughed like no tomorrow. A deceitful building that one was, a deadly trickster, a caster of spells, that made them believe they were destined for one another.

The Sister orders a double Black Jack, straight up. The Handler has a soda with lime, and Ronnie a Virgin Mary. Ronnie wishes to become the slats of shiny, polyurethane-coated wood that make up the table top. Or he could be a coaster, a useful, protective item.

The Sister tosses back her drink and gestures for another. Her face is a mask flawlessly framed by her habit. She has hands, but no continuous body anyone can see. She looks directly at Ronnie for the first time since she cast him to the depths of hell.

Whata matta, baby boy, she says. *You've gone all quiet.*

Silence gives consent, the Handler says.

The frailty of it all, the Sister says, *that's what so disappointing, isn't it? It does seem impossible that all those immaculate experiences, those intensities can flash up on the screen and disappear. How can there be that strict division between what is and what won't be? I traveled once to find my former lives, but they had vanished. All those gestures. All those moving shadows. Gone. Yes, but I know know know they still wait somewhere, even if only for my acknowledgement. Just to be recognized. Just to be accepted. Don't you see? But anyway, you're right. Silence is the answer. Sad to say, though, we're not good at making silence. We don't know how. It's too scary first of all. And then you have the little problem that even languages are mortal, and words are all we have. It's just like scenes making up a movie, isn't it? The latest one referring to the one before and the one before referring to the one that's next, and before them all, and after, nothing. There are twelve whole days of Christmas, and how many days of a video store, and how many scenes in those days? Betcha,* she says, leaning in close enough to Ronnie for him to smell the flowers of bourbon living in her breath, *those mucky, shiny, all-exhilarating scenes are only there to get between us and the Big Show, which we get to play in but can't ever see. So cheer up, baby boy. The movie probably comes out fine in the end.*

Clairvoyance

Some people pursue unhappiness like a quest. That's okay. You have to find a way to spend your time. But Felice was not like that.

Felice was famous when she was a child. Her family lived in DC at that time, and she was singled out to attend the annual Easter Egg Roll on the White House lawn. As she pushed an egg with the long spoon she had been given, the President's dog ran up and bit her on the ankle. The Secret Service came and put the dog on a leash and led it away. Then the President came and sat down in the grass by her and put her on his lap. The bite didn't break the skin and didn't hurt that much but she was crying. Cry-ing. That's what she was doing in her big moment, in the picture that appeared in newspapers and magazines and on TVs all across the country, while the President consoled her.

The President comforts Janice Lutz, 7, after Bonzo's bite, the caption in *The Washington Post* said. Her mother cut the picture out and put it in a scrapbook.

The commentators said it was a good moment for the President, that it really turned things around for him. Some even claimed it was what got him re-elected.

That doesn't happen to every little girl, her mother told her at the time.

And sure enough, nothing that special had happened to her since, but it didn't matter. She had kind of already had her peak experience and gotten it out of the way, and everything else was gravy. Sometimes she could still feel the itchy fabric of the President's pants touching her skin below her Easter dress.

This event from her youth gave her an independent streak, like a gift. Some people feel that they have gifts and go around worrying whether they're using their gifts or not, like a gift is really just an obligation. But she used her gift of independence all the time, without ever thinking about it. She wasn't particularly looking for happiness or unhappiness, or feeling compelled to achieve something great, or waiting for anything to happen. She could move freely through the world. She understood that history was too big to be considered real, and was only a big story that was always getting bigger. But she was the reason a President was re-elected, which meant she had a place in the story, no matter how big it ever got. She was an actual character, not just an anonymous participant. Still, she wasn't hung up about the President's dog thing and didn't tell people about it to make herself special.

But strange things kept happening, and she wondered about them sometimes like a mystery. A neighbor in the next apartment, an old guy, had a dog that looked exactly like the President's dog. When the old guy moved to the nursing home, even though they had never really talked, he asked her to take over the dog, like he knew she and the dog were connected. The dog was old too. He would sleep all day and then suddenly wake up and stagger around like he was receiving signals from another planet. When she said his name he listened like it was the name of a dog he used to know, and just stood there. But when she changed his name to Bonzo, the name of the President's dog, he came right away, gradually, to that name every time! Before long she moved to a new building where there weren't any old people, and the dog died. A creek bed ran behind the building and sometimes at night she heard a high yip-yip-yapping sound down there with a Doppler effect, coming and going. The guy in the next apartment claimed it was coyotes. He said they were eating people's cats. Right in the city! And that's history for you. You can memorize all the presidents and wars you want, but there will always be something weird running down the middle of it, that nobody can really explain. Because the coyote guy, a globular, baggy T-shirt person who hung around her in this hopeless I fantasize that I'm your boyfriend way, thought she might be lonely when the old dog died, though she wasn't, and got her another dog that looked exactly the same, and she pretty much had to give the new dog the same name.

The name provided a nice continuity in her life and connected the dogs, as well. She firmed up these ideas about connections while working at her very first job, at Perpetual Pets, a crematorium that turned people's dogs and cats into ashes they could keep forever. After the cremations, she swept the ashes into a plastic bag with a whisk broom and put the bag in the urn the customer had chosen. There were metal urns that looked like trophies and ceramic urns in the shape of a cat or dog, but most people chose a wooden urn, a box really, with a small brass plaque that displayed the pet's name. Sometime the ashes got a little mixed up, which was inevitable, and added bits of the cremains of other dogs and cats together with the pet named on the urn, like friends-in-perpetuity. The President is dead. The dog on the White House lawn and the dog who woke up suddenly are dead. Are they still connected?

The answer has to be *Yes* because, if for no other reason, Felice and the original Bonzo, and by extension the President, were connected in fame. The next big national crisis following the dog bite was over Bonzo's fate. Would the President put the dog down now that he had started attacking children? There were campaigns on both sides, with supporters of the dog death penalty going up against the Save Bonzo people, who ran ads with cute pictures of Bonzo's face in a kind of pleading pose when he was probably asking for a dog biscuit. Polls showed that seventeen percent more people wanted to save Bonzo than to kill him. The President waited until the campaigns reached a frenzy and then went on TV and pardoned Bonzo, commuting the death penalty to life in house arrest, away from White House visitors. The decision boosted the President's approval rating higher than it had ever been before, and made even more people aware of the Egg Roll bite because the networks kept playing the video of it, with Bonzo charging up in slow motion and a little white circle superimposed around Felice's ankle at the moment of impact.

Felice knew that a faint odor of fame still clung to her, which people could barely perceive and could not place in any particular context. This was not a big deal but it could be unsettling. There was no evidence that it put people off, but a lot of things transpire without any evidence. Also, she knew the truth, which is that though her fame was not terribly old compared to really old things, it still came from a gone world, like from a cemetery, which a lot of people don't want to think about. The current President didn't even have a dog. Besides, think how impossible it is to remember all the famousness you encounter in your lifetime. All the sitcoms, assassinations, super groups, super bowls, pandemics, scandals, social media celebrities, mass shootings, tsunamis, and best supporting actors. It can smother you or paralyze you or at least take a long time to think about when you could be doing something else. The larger than life thing. That is the burden of fame.

To cut herself loose a little from that burden, and also because she had never really cared for the name Janice, Janice used her gift of independence and changed her name to Felice. Also, she moved halfway 'cross the country from DC.

Felice, her mother said, when she told her, on the phone. *Felice,* she said again, like she was tasting it. Then she said *I'd kind of like it if it didn't sound like the name of a subversive. And if it didn't and I liked it better than Janice I would have named you that in the first place.*

It's possible her parents named her after Janis Joplin, they were always vague about that. They could at least have spelled it like she did. But what is a Janice, aside from Jan-is Joplin? Pretty much a no-thing, like being a tree instead of an elm or a pine, or a can with a label that just says Beans.

Now Felice cuts hair for a living. She chose haircutting because she wanted a profession that did not make major deductions from her life. Also, she had a gift for it. Also, cutting hair is like being a therapist or bartender, with fewer deductions. After you cut somebody's hair a few times you know pretty much everything about them, except things they might be hiding, and even those things you can kind of see. People think they're good at hiding, but they're not. Also, cutting hair is everything about appearances. Hair, clothes: a look you can change anytime. Surf-ace. It's a great place to live, because you can see everything, and if you sink down below it you're lost. It's where you can't get smothered or paralyzed. That's the thing, because it's arbitrary. It may be arranged by somebody and that somebody only happens to exist. So. It's rollerskates.

Old surf-ace won't ask you for anything. You can live there, and skate all you want, and know there are vast expanses hidden from you and weird things running down the middle of your life, and skate right on. Thinking too much about it doesn't help.

Which is why Felice didn't aspire to own a salon or anything like that. Instead she rented a chair in somebody else's salon where she was the only haircutter with a barber's license as opposed to a cosmetologist's license, which meant she was the only one who could give a guy a shave. Actually she kind of specialized in guys. They were mostly easy. Some people have this tender, complicating thing about their hair, like it wants to misrepresent them in some way. Felice's customers were not like that.

For romance, she mostly dated her customers. This was natural because during a haircut you talked about this and that and you pretty much knew what was up or wasn't, and you caught eyes in the mirror that told you whatever else. It wasn't a method, it was just a course of events that beat the dust off actual methods like online dating, which might be certifiably insane, and going out to bars, which was cheesy. Sometimes she slept with the customers she dated and sometimes she didn't. To keep things uncomplicated, she dated one guy at a time, and mostly single guys, even though the married ones might have a little more to offer than the singles, which is why somebody married them in the first place. On the other hand, the married ones might have the guilt thing or the you listen while I talk about my marriage thing. That was their problem. Whatever, her relationships tended to move like the Doppler effect, in one direction from I hear you coming to I can't hear you at all. She wasn't good, especially, at maintenance. Checkout time would come and that was it. She was good at picking guys who could understand when it was over, so mostly the boyfriend customers remained in her chair even after they had stopped being boyfriends. Of course this took skill to manage, but it wasn't anything she had to earn. It was more like a gift. When checkout time came she might drop hints like putting backslashes in her text messages to the guy in question. \\\\\ *Great*!, if you knew how to read it, was thank you and goodbye.

She didn't fall in love. Her parents fell in love with each other and then fell in love with other people. People she knew were always falling in love with somebody or something they did or somewhere they had gone or wanted to go, or wanting to be in love if they weren't, like being hungry and having to eat. Whatever they loved owned them, pretty much. Felice didn't feel it. The love thing was not all that necessary, at the end of the day. If you wanted people hanging around you could figure out how to have them. And if you went looking for them, they were either attractive in some way or not, interesting or interested or not, no smothering and no paralysis. That was the thing. She wasn't anti-love. You had to find a way to spend your time. She even had a philosophy about it. Not loving anything or anybody in particular, she thought, was more or less like loving everything, with no possession or jealously or insecurity over whether that thing you loved so much loved you. It was truly pure.

Right now she was dating Sad Bob. Bob went sad the day he found out he was a white guy. Before that he was a Native American, and that was more or less his whole thing. But he called himself an Indian, or sometimes an *American* Indian to distinguish from an Indian from India. He said an Indian could call himself an Indian, that was his privilege, but that white guys damn sure better call him a Native American if they didn't want to go to war. Then one day he made a bad choice and spit into a vial and sent it off to find out just how pure Indian he was. And he wasn't. He was mostly Irish and a couple of other white things. So he had to call what he used to be a Native American, and he hadn't gotten over it.

Sad Bob was a fairly good-looking guy who had been a customer a long time. He had long black hair with a little bit of natural wave to it that went way down his back and that he mostly wore in a ponytail. Sometimes he stuck a feather in it. You wouldn't think there would be much reason for a haircut if you wore your hair that way, and there wasn't. Sad Bob liked a barbershop shave. He said his Dad, who people called Chief—which Bob explained would have been an insult to an Indian if his Dad hadn't actually been the Police Chief in the town—got a barbershop shave every morning. It was his only luxury, Bob claimed, and it meant something to him. And little Bob would sit in one of the chairs below the row of mirrors across from the barber's chairs in the old-timey barbershop where the whole place smelled like Bay Rum and watch the shave go on, and that was a good memory. But he himself didn't get a shave every day because he didn't have time due to his job, just every few weeks, when he would come in with a stand of rough fuzz on his face. He didn't have enough facial hair to support a full beard, but he could raise a pretty good moustache that

he was proud of. He was the only customer who took advantage of
Felice's Barber's License, which made him stand out. It was kind of
fun to do a shave, so Felice looked forward to Bob's appointments
even though he wouldn't let her trim his eyebrows, which were world
travelers, or the moustache, which usually needed it bad.

The day Bob found out he wasn't an Indian anymore he came in
looking like a truck had run over his dog and then backed up and run
over it again, and he sat down in the chair and looked into the mirror at Felice and told her to cut it off. Cut it all off. And of course he
meant his hair. And she did, and he actually was a lot better looking
without it, which she told him but it didn't cheer him up. He wasn't
just a white guy, he said, he was a white guy who had lost his faith. By
which he meant his faith in his Dad who he more or less worshipped
and who was the one who told him about being an Indian when he was
little, and gave him the gift of his Indian dream with a teepee in the
backyard and a headdress for the war dance. Maybe his Dad really was
a Native American, like he claimed, and maybe since Sad Bob knew
the truth about his genes his Dad wasn't Sad Bob's Dad after all, which
just made the whole thing worse. And now his Dad had died and there
was nobody to see about it.

And then he said take off the moustache too, and trim the eyebrows way down, and he was even better looking and even more sad.

The only thing he had left was his job, he said, the one thing in life
he really cared for, Indian or not. He worked as a medical tech for a
cardiologist, attaching electrodes to people's chests to look into their
hearts and see if they were pure and open or clogged up and nasty,
and if Felice ever asked him what was going on at work he tended to
talk about the equipment that he used, not about the people he connected the electrodes to. People were heart muscles to him and blips
on a screen, which were either good blips or bad blips or no blips if he
had to figure out why the machinery wasn't working or if the patient
died during a stress test after running on the treadmill, which had

happened only once so far. He was geeky in that way.

When Felice took the smock off his shoulders he stood up on the river of his hair that ran in currents on the white tile floor, and caught her eyes in the mirror like the moment had suddenly spilled over on all sides with meaning and asked her if she would go out with him that night, for dinner or whatever. Felice noticed he was a little on the short side, and wondered why she hadn't seen that before. She had just broken it off with Worried Paul, a tall, thin guy with thin, straight hair that just wanted to lie down and rest. Paul worried about death. It wasn't that his life had been particularly great or shown a special promise, he said, though he had no major complaints. He just felt kind of responsible and didn't want to cause a hardship by not being around to watch things happen, for better or for worse. Recently he had become hopeful because of Pindar. Pindar thought you might go to hell if you weren't careful but that the goddess Persephone was in charge of recycling souls there. She would run your soul through a program where it was rehabilitated in the way it needed and then send it back out in a new body to try again. Felice thought Paul's discouraged hair might have something to do with all his worry. The break-up had gone really well and Paul was cool with still being a customer. So she looked back into Sad Bob's eyes in the mirror and said *Why not?*

I'm a new man, by God, Sad Bob said, *whether I like it or not.* He paid with a Visa card and left.

Felice did not indulge in expectations. Expectations, she believed, were for people who wanted to add a sense of efficiency to their lives by knowing what will happen, so they don't have to waste time waiting to find out. It was cheating, in a way. She didn't need efficiency and wasn't really an efficient person. People wouldn't say that about her. She might have a dress draping the microwave and shoes in the hamper, but she knew where things were. There was no point in setting things in some fixed order as if they wouldn't change on their own. In addition to the dog, she hosted a colony of truly tiny ants—smaller than gnats, she thought, though she hadn't measured—who left messages on the kitchen countertop. They formed themselves into letters that were completely distinct though never quite still. There was a different sequence of letters every morning. Felice wasn't surprised that she couldn't make sense of them. There were all kinds of languages, and she only knew one. Still, she felt quite solid about things. She wasn't one of those people who look like they'll fall apart if you touch them. She didn't need self-help books. Before the salon door closed behind Sad Bob, she had visualized her wardrobe, selected an outfit for the night, put it on, changed it, and changed it again. Then the next customer arrived and without Felice even asking, started telling her how his daughter had made another disastrous decision in her love life.

They drove their own cars to the restaurant. Sad Bob got there first. When she came in, he had to step in front of her because she was looking past him, which is understandable due to the fact that he was smaller than previous Bob, differently oriented to the world, jumpier and possibly built on entirely different genes, though he wore the same leather bombardier-style jacket. Felice wondered if he was connected to a different fate. She was pretty sure that changing from Janice to Felice had done that for her, in a good way.

Sad Bob had chosen a middle-of-the-road kind of place, not cheap, not fancy. It served locally-raised food. People who ate there thought of themselves as good people, but it was not a place that looked back at you like it knew what it was and wondered if you knew the same about yourself. It was just boards and paint, like a stage set for a play, with gas stoves and sinks hidden in the back. A hostess showed them to a booth. Over drinks, Sad Bob gave Felice another one of those meaningful looks like the one from the mirror in the salon, but the mirror was missing and this time the look slipped into funny in an unfortunate way. Probably Bob had always had doggie eyes, loyal brown and extra expressive, but the trimmed eyebrows helped Felice notice them for the first time. *Don't make any sudden moves,* the eyes said. Then they said *Please.*

He took a drink and kept looking at her over the top of his glass, like giving the full mysteriousness of the mystery time to settle in. An ice cube dropped out of the glass and into his lap. He brushed it off. *You may not believe this,* Bob said, *but I knew we would get together.* He waited to gauge Felice's reaction but there wasn't any. *It's weird but I knew it, I did. When I was an Indian I could see things, like a path with road signs that don't have any words or arrows but still tell you which way to go if you can understand them, which most people can't. Like say I might be watching a game, and I might know who would win. Not just because one side had the best team or when the score was already lopsided, but right in the middle when it was really close. It wouldn't come like a sentence made of words, it was just a certitude. Usually when I got that feeling I was right. I missed on almost all the big important stuff, but I pretty much knew some things. The thing about you and me I knew for sure and certain, solid as this.*

He knocked his knuckles on the table. It was pretty clear he wanted his certitude to mean something.

You really do look different, Felice said.

A new man, Bob said bitterly. He ordered another round and glanced quickly out across the restaurant as though he were being watched. Then with his eyes fixed periodically on Felice's, Sad Bob confessed his romantic history. He had been through a couple of live-ins but never married. The first live-in was a drug addict who didn't love Sad Bob. She only wanted him for the Percocet and OxyContin he could bring her because of where he worked. She told lies as a religious practice. The second live-in probably did love him, he thought. But she was so depressed she couldn't get out of bed most days, so her participation in the relationship was limited, which depressed her even more, so much that she had to leave. Despite these life experiences, Sad Bob believed that when the right woman came along he would know it, *gut know it*. He wouldn't have to check off boxes on a questionnaire. He hadn't given up on everything, not yet, but he did have some adjustments to make and he figured that might take a while. And obviously the right woman would be a different woman now than she would have been before, since he was a new man.

I'm lost, he said, and emptied his drink.

He looked satisfied, there on his side of the booth, like being lost was an achievement. The waiter came and Sad Bob told him they would wait a while to order food. They did the getting to know you thing over several more rounds of drinks, talked about what they liked and didn't like in the categories of vegetables and noises. Felice liked sirens. They were a good example of the Doppler effect and they were kind of exciting. Bob rejected the entire notion of cauliflower. Then they went back into their childhoods and covered candy and cartoons. They got a little drunk. Then they ate and got full and sleepy. Sad Bob played with the salt and pepper shakers.

I wanted to go on a vision quest, Sad Bob said. *Guess it's too late now.* He tried to laugh but nothing came out.

Felice leaned back in the corner of the booth, sliding down a little. *What if it's all a vision?* she said, and Sad Bob blinked. *And it just goes rowww-ling by. But! It rolls by you. Whatever it is, it's yours. And if everybody saw it,* she said, *like some big crowd, you still have your own special share. Like the siren going by. Or like if a dog runs up and bites you.*

I really hate the noise leaf blowers make, Sad Bob said. *But I had a dog when I was a kid. My best friend.*

Felice didn't ask what kind of dog. They didn't talk about what they would do next. What they did was, they took an Uber to Sad Bob's place. Everything was put away and tidy there, the bed was tightly made, the pillows fluffed. There were purple tulips in a vase on the bar. It was like the model unit for the complex, all staged to generate the perfect first impression. Bob gave Felice a messy kiss but she could tell his heart wasn't in it. She understood. As part of her gift of independence, she could get other people's feelings without catching them. It doesn't mean not caring, it just introduces a useful element of objectivity.

They undressed and got in bed, and lay there looking up at the ceiling. It was a nice moment, not really peak on the experience scale, but easy to be around. She closed her eyes and dozed a bit. Maybe she said it out loud and maybe she didn't.

I'm thinking of changing my name, is what she may have said. *I wonder what it might be.*

Sparkle!

Claude gets the news about Shirley from Denise. Which is strange because Shirley is, was, his high school sweetheart and Denise is the woman he married. Plus, Denise never met Shirley. She only accompanied Claude to a couple of high school reunions where Shirley was present as a Missing Person, when someone would ask about her and there was never any news. And for a kicker, there are Shirleys all over the house, and a dedicated Shirley room across the landing from their bedroom, because Denise is nuts for Shirley Temple dolls.

Claude is watching a game or reading, what have you, and looks at his watch and it's past 1AM. He goes down to the spare bedroom Denise uses as an office and there she is in the dark with just the glow of the screen coming through her hair and leaking around her shoulders like a poltergeist. She says why pay for electricity you don't need, which he gets, but still.

You think you'll come to bed? He asks.

He knows Shirley Temple has her weird always-open eyes on him, even though he can just see her silhouette. She sits right there on the desk by the computer, all dimples and sausage curls, propped up on a doll stand with her legs splayed out in front of her. She's eighty years old and made of composition, which is glue mixed with sawdust, and she cost twelve hundred bucks. The composition Shirleys are the ones everybody wants.

Isn't this the one you dated in high school? Denise says, *the one whose heart you claim you broke?*

So there's a picture on Facebook, the brightest thing in the room, and it looks more or less like he remembers Shirley. Yes, Shirley used to perm her hair. He doesn't do Facebook, but Denise is hooked. She's got her own page and a Hello Shirley Temple Dolly page, and her Shirley's Collection Corner YouTube channel, and about a million friends and subscribers.

She was married to a quadriplegic, Denise says.

Well gosh, he says. *What happened? Did he get sick or have an accident, or what?*

How I am supposed to know that?

You know the guy's a quadriplegic.

Denise makes her *pfffffh* sound, there in the dark.

You can make light of it now because it's locked up in the past, but Claude and Shirley were pretty serious at one point, as serious as things can be when you're eighteen. They came up in a roughneck town on the coast, oil rigs and chemical plants lit up in the night with smoke pouring from them like the fortress of an underworld queen. The tap water smelled like rotten eggs. They would drive down to the beach and get all over each other on a blanket in the dunes, with the wind whipping them on and a soundtrack of waves concussing on the shore. And Claude did break her heart, he admits. He's not proud of it like Denise makes it sound. She doesn't even know the worst part, which was the way he talked about it to his friends, and the way they talked about it so that everybody knew, and Shirley quit coming to school. Years later he ran into Shirley's big sister and she told him to his face he had *ruined Shirley's life.* Aside from that nobody in her family would say boo to him if they saw him on the street, not that he really made an effort. He went off to the Navy and she went off to beauty college and he never laid eyes on her again until that night on the screen.

So, are we going to the funeral? Denise asks.

That had not occurred to Claude. It's an interesting part of being married a long time. Denise comes up with things he might have thought or maybe should have thought, but didn't. His impulse is to say no, it's been too long. The idea scares him a little to tell the truth, who knows what could come up there even if it might be the right thing to do, but he's still kind of curious about it and kicking it around when Denise says *It's not that far. We should go.*

He bends closer to look at the thread on the screen and it really isn't that far. Maybe ten miles. Which is strange. Shirley and Claude leave their hometown halfway across Texas, and he goes off all over the world, and who knows where all she goes, and they end up right down the road from one another. Maybe they're that close for years and never know it. Maybe they pass each other on a toll road or push carts down parallel aisles in the Home Depot, like chunks of space junk that used to be part of the same planet. Maybe they sit in the same movie theater on the same row and laugh at the same joke.

Three days and three nights go by. The days are like all days and the nights are like all nights.

The morning of the funeral, Claude polishes his good dress shoes and worries that he'll pop the waist button off his black suit, or not be able to draw a breath. Denise does her hair and tries on three or four outfits like she does every time she thinks she might be viewed by anybody but him, and meanwhile he waits downstairs in his favorite red leather chair all suited up, with his dress belt let out a notch and the waist button left open. He can hear Denise above him, walking back and forth from her closet to the mirror. Right there at his elbow on an end table beside a purple orchid is a porcelain Shirley dressed in a pink pinafore. Sometimes his mind wanders. He daydreams what his life might have been with Shirley if he hadn't dumped her for Liesel, the exchange student who turned right around and dumped him. And if he hadn't shot his mouth off bragging to his buds. He doesn't get far with those dreams because people who are eighteen are only half-baked and how can you make sense of what they might be like at 35 or 50 or even 72, except by then you know one of them is dead, and also, it feels kind of like a rejection of his whole actual life to have those thoughts. So he wonders for a minute about all the missing parts of Shirley's life he doesn't know, which are most of them. He thinks maybe he can learn some of that at the funeral, talk to someone who knew her or listen to the eulogy, whatever, at least get a glimpse of her the way she ended up. Then he starts remembering how it was when he and Shirley had sex, and thinking how it might have been if they'd done some of the things they didn't know about at the time, and that becomes a detour he can't turn loose of. He's got this quasi boner poking up against his suit pants when Denise calls down asking if he's ready, like she has been waiting on him. That is a rare event these days, the boner not the calling down, and he's enjoying it, though it might be wrong to fantasize that way about a dead person when you treated her like a bastard and you're about to leave for her funeral with your wife. When Denise descends the stairs he stands up and turns to the window like he has just spotted a hummingbird on the feeder. Denise goes into the kitchen to fill her water bottle and by the time she calls out again, telling him he's going to make them late, he's somewhat presentable.

Turns out they are late. It's the GPS and not Claude, though you couldn't tell it from the atmospheric pressure in the car. *To be on time is to be late,* Denise likes to say. It's one of her things. The funeral home has a big parking lot with a total of one van in it, and a hearse way at the back. It's a bright, hot day.

Inside, they cross an empty lobby to a door with a sign that says Chapel. You'd think those kind of places would have quiet, deferential doors that don't call attention to themselves. This one is made to look like the portal to King Tut's tomb. It's so heavy or so stuck Claude thinks it's locked at first, but he gives it a good jerk and it slams open with a sound pretty close to a gunshot that echoes off the walls.

The chapel is empty except for a knot of people around a casket at the very front, who jump at the sound and jerk their heads toward it. Three little living worlds, and one world in a box that has already turned to stone and started up orchards of crystal and bacteria and taken off through space looking to discover gravity anywhere it can. That's the crowd, a man and woman standing and another man seated in a motorized chair. The casket lid is open right behind them, and a spray of flowers is lashed to an easel off to the side.

Claude and Denise step in and the door waits a couple beats and fires again behind them. As the echo dies down they hear organ chords spieling out from hidden speakers. Even though it's a good-size chapel, with a comfortable number of rows of pews between them and the front, they can smell the tuberoses. They don't want to shake things up any more so they take seats in the back row.

Claude notices the standing woman hasn't ever turned back around. She's staring at him so hard he feels the radiation across all that empty space. She mouths some kind of curse. Then she bends down to the guy in the chair and whispers something in his ear. The chair makes a noise like a big zipper coming open and spins in a 180, and now there's two of them staring. The other guy glances for just a second. Whatever's going on, he doesn't get it.

The woman starts to move like she's coming for Claude, but the guy in the chair says something to her and she stops. They stare another half minute and then they turn back around to the casket and kind of huddle up.

It turns out the standing guy is the preacher. He goes up some steps to a pulpit. By now Claude has figured out that the woman has to be Shirley's big sister, even though she looks nothing like he remembers. She's twice the size and all crinkled and sour. He's not the boy he was back then either. He doesn't know how she recognizes him. She takes an aisle seat on the front row and the chair guy parallel parks beside her.

The preacher is a mumbler. Maybe there's a microphone but it isn't turned on. It's like nobody wants the back row to know the secrets you tell corpses in their coffins. After a respectful period of nothing Claude takes Denise's hand and they shoot off the door a couple of times on their way out.

Claude doesn't drive away. He moves to a patch of shade on the side of the lot and sits there with the air conditioner running. A cop car is parked over by the hearse.

What? Denise says.

I thought we might go to the graveyard.

You think those people want you there?

We'll stay way off. Otherwise there won't be anybody.

Denise makes her *wheeeww* sound that is almost a whistle, but she just gets out her phone and sits there in communication with the screen.

After a while, across the lot, some guys come out with the casket and load it in the hearse. The husband drives his chair onto a lift that puts him in the van. It's pretty cool the way it happens. The hearse lines up behind the cop car and the sister gets into the driver's seat of the van and pulls over behind the hearse. Claude hangs back a couple of blocks behind the little procession.

At the cemetery he parks on a narrow road that runs right down the middle and watches the guys unpack the casket and the same clutch of three figures form beside the grave. They're a good ways off, but Claude can see the preacher is reading from the Bible. Denise is done with the funeral and whoever she's texting with is making her laugh. The funeral home has put up a shade with some rows of empty chairs under it. Sometimes when you watch a scene like that off in the distance for a while, especially across a crop of headstones with the light kind of dusty and hot, you might wonder if it's real. The figures are so still and small, just smudgy representatives of people, and you can't hear anything. What if somebody has staged the whole deal, to scam the insurance or for a really sick prank? Claude shakes his head as he drives off.

On the highway, he sees a sign for a motel and takes the exit. Denise looks up.

Pit stop? She says.

Know what, Claude says. *I'm just thinking it's hot and there's some kind of swimming pool right over there. And we don't really have to be anywhere. Remember when we first started out?*

If you mean the dumps where you took me, I do.

Ha ha, he says, *no, I'm just thinking we have a swim, a nice dinner, take it easy and go on home tomorrow. Change of scenery.*

A motel room is your idea of scenery?

Claude shrugs. He doubts that she will play along, but what the hell.

We're halfway home now, and we don't have any suits, Mr. Spontaneity. What are we supposed to swim in?

He hadn't thought of that, but doesn't say so. Instead he stays on the frontage until the next turnaround and drives back to the Walmart he noticed across the highway, like that had been his plan all along. And they buy suits. Denise doesn't like hers. He tells her it looks great, though it's not really flattering, and points out that no one knows them at this pool and she can throw it out on the highway or leave it in the room for the maid if she doesn't want to take it home. He's happy, he gets that way. He can see she's kind of getting into the swing of it too, though she acts like it's the craziest idea he's ever had. It's been forever since they did anything like this.

They change in the room. The pool is small but they have it to themselves. A sign advises that no life guard is on duty. Wading down the steps, Claude is surprised by the waves bouncing up against him, throwing back needles of sunshine. It's like somebody has jumped into the deep end to swim with them, but they didn't because he looks over that way and there's nobody there. He even waits a few seconds to see if they surface but they never do. Claude leans against the side with a little bit of vertigo. One of the waves lifts up a drowned wasp in front of him like a cracker on a plate and he scoops it up and lets the water run through his fingers. He takes the wasp over and sets it on the corner of the pool and it starts flopping around, or trying to, because it's on its back. So he takes a leaf and fools with it until it kind of grabs hold and he tries to turn it over. He has to do that a couple of times before it's standing up. But now it looks like it only has one wing, or maybe its wings are stuck together and it keeps falling on its side. He figures it's a goner, but he did what he could.

A hell of a thing, Denise says. He kind of jumps because she's standing right there behind him in the shallow end. The water is barely rumpled.

I know, he says.

Not your bug, she says. *Your girl Shirley. Wasted there in a box from every kind of cancer and all those empty pews. Didn't she know anybody? And that poor man in the chair. Jesus. The lives people live, and we still pray to God! But what the hell for? Who do we think is listening?*

I don't know if you can put it all on God, Claude says, and Denise gives him a smirk. He's still not feeling exactly perfect, and it takes him a minute to chase down what he's going to say. He puts his elbows up behind him on the side of the pool. *I mean God's been busy since day one, running after every living thing. He's probably exhausted, and then He comes along and it's like there's this drowning bug but it's too late and nothing can be done. It doesn't mean He doesn't care.*

You've got yourself all mixed up with God, Denise says. *That's your problem.*

And he gets what she's saying, it's terrible what happened to Shirley, but the next time he looks over at the side of the pool the wasp is gone.

They don't swim long, and it's too hot to sit in the chairs. After they shower and change they get dinner in the restaurant attached to the motel. It's not the swankiest, but better than you might expect. Shades on the windows make it dark and candles float in little cups. It's still early and they're the only people there.

Let's live it up, Claude says as they sit down. *Have whatever we desire.* Which they would anyway—why cheap out at this point?—but it feels good to say it. Claude has the flounder. Denise has the nicoise. They split a warm fudge ala mode.

They're walking back to the room and Denise says *Why don't we just drive home? We're almost there, and we can sleep in our own bed.*

It's not exactly the idea Claude had, but that's okay. They took a little break, had a little fun. Romance is problematic at a certain point and you can't always hit it on the button, and anyway the edge has kind of gone off things. They get in the car and Claude takes his time on the road. They hold hands on the console. The last little bit of sunset peekaboos between the buildings.

Claude's mind begins to slip, to fly and land badly. He's driving his old Dodge with his free arm wrapped around Shirley, on the way to the beach, making fun of his high school football coach and driving instructor: *Both eyes on the road, both hands on the wheel.* But somebody else is talking. It's Denise, reminding him she leaves tomorrow on a trip to Santa Fe with her sister and her niece. *It's good to have some time away,* she says, *and good for you too, a few days on your own.* Claude is glad when they make it home.

While Denise is gone, the world is made new each night and each day. The surfaces of things are unfamiliar. The under-surfaces are skeptical of Claude's existence.

The first morning behaves like it is off to a good start. Claude's bud Frank has been after him to help out with the restoration of an old Corvette, and that takes up some time. But otherwise Claude's life is not his own. From his cereal and coffee, from the T-bones at the butcher counter and the dialog in reruns on the Hallmark Channel, a mist of Shirley thoughts rises up to ambush Claude. Demonized inventions interrupt his attention. Shadows sit him up in bed. A restlessness sears him and paces him about.

Finally a plan occurs to him, but he's not sure if he came up with it or it was lying there in wait for him, like a path in a jungle. It doesn't feel like any plan he's ever made. But that's okay because having any kind of plan helps with the jitters or whatever it is.

He climbs the stairs up to the Shirley room.

He hardly ever goes in there unless he's looking for Denise, so it's a little weird, like walking through a neighbor's house when they aren't home. The first thing he sees is the framed photograph on the dresser, an 8 x 10 Denise bought at a Doll Swap and Expo. Shirley prays. Her chubby, manicured fingers spire up beneath her chin, and her too big, too round eyes roll up to heaven. She wears lipstick and mascara. The legend is that the inscription on the picture was written by Shirley's Momma. It says *Sparkle!* That's what Momma tells Shirley every time she prances off onto a film set for the next take, or poses for a session of publicity stills. Thanks to Denise, Claude is more or less a storehouse of Shirley info. He knows Shirley Temple has exactly fifty-six golden ringlets. She has to have her hair rinsed in vinegar and set in pin curls every night. At three, she plays Morelegs Sweetrick in the Baby Burlesques shorts, trading kisses for lollypops with actors in diapers. At four, she is a call girl who becomes the mistress of a diapered Senator in a movie called *Polly Tix in Washington*.

The shelves lined with Shirleys are on full alert, following the intruder's every move. Birthday Shirley from the Danbury Mint, toting a cake with five candles; Texas Centennial Shirley in boots, leather chaps and vest, with her hat raked back on her curls and the pin on her bandana that says *The World's Darling*; toddler Shirley; hard plastic Shirley; saltware Shirley; flirty eye Shirley; chorus lines of paper doll Shirleys; the tall Shirley Claude calls Psycho who has acted life-size in his dreams; sleepy Shirley; Shirley that looks more like Martha Washington; Shirley books, cups, pitchers, plates, bowls, pocket mirrors, music boxes, and million dollar bills; and inside the dresser, spare Shirleys, Shirley heads and body parts, drawers full of Shirley's clothes and socks and shoes.

He pulls open the top drawer where Denise keeps her minor league Shirleys and picks out a nude vinyl model with rouged-up cheeks, one he thinks maybe Denise won't miss for a while. Her eyes come open as he lifts her. She's a little beat up, nicked here and there, but there is distance and intent in the way she watches him, responds to his touch and knows her purpose. He selects a powder blue Party Doll dress with flouncy sleeves and a sewn-in slip, puts her in it with difficulty because his fingers are a size too large, tugs up her panties carefully, slips on a pair of butterfly socks and black ankle strap shoes. She's not exactly what he wanted but she looks pretty good.

He takes her up and holds her in his arms like a baby and carries her downstairs. Shows her all around the house, the back yard, his tools in the garage, narrating the scenes where life has landed him, like a tour guide. Finally he gets a ballpoint and a pad from the desk in the front hall and settles down with her in his chair. He and his Shirley would be alone in the house except for the porcelain Shirley beside them, the Shirleys populating every nook, judging every effort and keeping tabs on every movement. He holds his own Shirley up to look at the porcelain Shirley, who is way too perfect, not like his. *She thinks she's such hot shit*, he says, or maybe he just thinks, or maybe it just runs through the room, that thought. He might have caught a little edge of a sneer on his own Shirley's face.

He props his Shirley beside him, writes a letter, wads it, writes the beginning of a eulogy, makes of it a paper airplane which he launches, draws a heart and writes a valentine, passes it to an open hand of dust motes and irregular sunshine. Behind each word is memory, in front of it, anticipation. As each submits into its bondage on the page, another fragment of the truth escapes. To end the misery he scratches out three words.

I'm sorry, Shirley, the words say.

With extra care he tears away the empty spaces of the page so it can be folded into doll size, and wedges it between his Shirley's thumb and forefinger. She holds it like a pro, a messenger. He goes back up to the Shirley room, picks up a Shirley pillow, and gets a big fluffy towel from the bathroom. They're ready to go.

Shirley sits upright in the passenger seat, staring at the glove compartment as he drives her to the cemetery. He struggles with a moment of disturbing happiness, and takes care not to speed. On the way, it occurs to him that Shirley might like to know some things that happened after they went their separate ways, in case she's curious.

He tells the Shirley in the car how he met Denise, on a blind date arranged by a buddy of his and his wife, at a pizza parlor near the first base where he was stationed, in San Diego. How they hit if off right away and got married before you could say boo.

He tells her things he possibly had told Denise but never told Shirley, of course, because he didn't know them when he knew her. Like the time the sailor standing next to him in the machine shop in the Philippines, at Subic Bay, whacked off his thumb on a table saw and Claude picked the thumb up off the floor and handed it to the guy, and the guy had a look on his face Claude couldn't forget and just said *Thanks*. And the Shirley never changes her expression but how could that matter?

At the cemetery, they walk to the place Claude remembers seeing from the car, the day of the funeral. He's pretty sure it's the right grave. The dirt is still mounded up. The flowers have surrendered and gone brown. Someone has put up a tombstone of manufactured black granite with no words on it. Claude drops to his knees supporting Shirley tenderly in both hands, her head on the pillow. After a minute he sets her aside and scoops out a well in the middle of the grave, deep enough and long enough. First he lays in the towel, then the pillow, then Shirley—who has closed her eyes—smooths the dress in places, and flicks a spec of dirt from her cheek. He thinks about vicissitudes. The weather, all that churns in the ground. Concludes that he's done what he can.

He swivels her arms to her sides, covers her with the remainder of the towel and shovels dirt with his hands until she's gone.

Back home Claude heats a frozen dinner, sleeps and rises. Mornings, evenings, afternoons, he suffers a peculiar exhaustion where nothing feels like anything. The air stuff he moves through is a heavy fluid.

One ordinary Tuesday in the brightest sun Claude is watering a sapling in his backyard when no one, nothing speaks to him in a voice he cannot hear. Does it say his name or someone else's? He will deny it speaks at all, though it cannot be denied. Is there something, everything incomprehensibly exacting in the bodies of Shirleys, that feints and defends and survives? He stands listening as water reaches for the ground. All he hears, all he sees are droplets striking cedar mulch, the standing tall stockade of his own privacy fence, the whisping-by of traffic, the familiar curtain of the world. Now he drops the hose and paces like a panther in a cage. Now he sits in a lawn chair in the shade with open palms until nothing calls again. There may have been no laughter. He goes to the garage, puts a hand on the door latch of the car, turns loose and re-enters the house. Nothing, no one on the line. Before he knows it he is back in the garage and in the car and burning down the highway, past the breaking-up pavement through a canyon of buildings that closes inward as he goes.

Shirley greets him at the grave. She's propped up against the headstone, her hands outstretched for him and empty, her blue party dress unblemished, fresh rouge on her cheeks, her curls shining clean. He stands there looking at her for a minute until he understands without a doubt she's looking back at him. Then he picks her up and holds her carefully.

I wanted the yellow dress, she says. *What took you so long?*

Claude looks around. Some people are putting a vase of flowers by a grave, way off in the distance.

I didn't see a yellow dress, he says.

It's right there at the other end of the drawer. All you have to do is use your eyes.

They get back in the car and talk all the way home. She says she doesn't really care for the shoes either, and the truth is she's always wanted to do something different with her hair. She doesn't like being touched by the creepy customers at doll shows, where she usually gets crammed in a bin with the cut-rate Shirleys. Claude tells her he prefers the people at the bowling alley and maybe he'll take her over there sometime.

They're a pretty good bunch, he says.

Denise comes home that night. Over breakfast the next day, she tells stories from the trip. That week she has bunco night and book club. Claude stows his Shirley in a sock drawer, underneath the wooly stuff that only comes out in the winter, where Denise doesn't poke around. He takes her out when Denise is away from the house. They try on different outfits. They watch TV. He holds her in his lap and they talk about whatever's going on with all the other Shirleys.

The Goat's Eye

We're screwing like squirrels in the laundry room, Chloe and I, knocking up against the front panel of Aunt Bug's new Maytag dryer so hard it complains like it's drying a bowling ball. I'm two years older, but I'm her uncle, more or less, and she's my niece, and we've both been hornier than toads for each other since puberty, which is forever to us but to the grand dance of time is nothing. Nothing at all.

It was fate that gave us our opportunity. The same bolt of fate that struck down old Great Aunt Bug left us unchaperoned on the musty lumps of her sofa in her parlour, the only room on the planet still called a parlour by any living human. First we sat close and then we sat closer and our arms touched and the short hairs of them tickled our skins into a bad case of goose pimples and our cheeks burned and we kissed and tongued and then we felt and then we stroked and then we started looking for a room where no one could bust in without a warning racket first and found the laundry. Which is in the cellar of Bug's wheezing, falling-down Victorian castle up on a mesa at the crown of her ranch. And which features a deadbolt on the door and two flights of intervening stairs between us and any of our relatives.

If you climb up in this house and look out from its turrets, you'll see emptiness every way you turn. It's a wilderness, but what isn't? You could run into Geronimo or John the Baptist or just about anybody out there. Terrain-wise, you're looking at high desert and mountains with giant eroded, human-featured figures, ghost stories made of rock, staring back at you on top. In those mountains there are caves and rock shelters with smoked ceilings and walls covered with red hand prints and pictures of bears, where you can pick up flint hide scrapers and arrow points and metates and all kinds of tools that go back ten thousand years. You have to be careful where you reach, especially in wintertime, because rattlers like to hibernate in those caves, but you can hold those tools in your hand and tell how they were used, and put the same hand up against that stone wall inside the hand print that is already there, that has been there waiting for you all that time. Those people had small hands, more like Aunt Bug's. When I was a kid I could pretty much fit my hand in theirs. Now my fingers spill out over the ones up on the wall.

If you pay attention on your perch you can watch a couple of roads made of packed dirt run off to nowhere and catch some movement from dust devils and tumbleweeds jumping like they're scared of getting shot. A ragged line of boulders big as dinosaurs stands out there for sentinels, and usually you'll spot a stack of buzzards in the air spiraling down on the latest thing that's died.

Nobody comes looking for us. Nobody hears the pounding on the Maytag, nobody is scandalized or outraged or titillated or even given the option of giving a good goddamn because every soul who might care is two floors away in the creepy, bric-a-brac festooned bedroom where Bug lies dying.

Chloe and I know for a simple fact that not one of the deathwatchers will leave that room prematurely for anything less than an Act of God Almighty, and then it better be a good one, because they all live in mortal, quaking awe of the little woman at the center of their diorama. At the present moment what they fear most is that if they dare to take their eyes off her unconscious form, she will rise up and call her lawyer to write them out of her will.

There's no telling how old Bug is, but it's not much either, in that grand dance I'm talking about. There are stones up in our mountains, I hear, that are 500 million years old. Compared to those stones, people aren't much a part of it. We've been here no time at all. It's only been 1,957 years since Jesus split a hymen from the inside out. Seems an odd way to measure time, but there it is. *How many years do you have*, is what the Mexicans say, like we own our time in this world. I've got nineteen, almost twenty. Chloe's got seventeen plus. I like the way she is alive. The way her mouth stays a little open. The high points of her cheeks are always a little pink, and her eyes always ready to laugh in some way that she keeps private. Right now her whole face has gone so red you can barely see the freckles. We've done all we can do to each other and we're both leaning on the dryer, buttoning up and breathing like horses in a derby. She puts her finger right on my breast bone, touching it through my shirt, and draws a little box and says *This is where we'll keep our secrets*. And now she does start laughing right out loud. She takes off up the cellar stairs and I go chasing after her, all rubber-legged, and we fall back on the sofa. We stare up at a sky of dark carved wood, way above our heads.

Who do you think she'll give it to? Chloe says.

I don't know and I don't care.

That might be a lie. *That is a lie*, Chloe tells me with a look.

I grew up on the ranch. I've worked it since I was old enough to ride. It's the only place I've ever known, so I can't tell you with a straight face that I don't care what happens to it. It's not right to say the ranch is part of me because it's too big to fit in me or anybody, but I'm sure part of it, as much as any creature out there dead or alive.

I don't remember when the two of us have been this still. We're just sitting with our heads thrown back, smelling thousand year old dust. We hear a door open and close on the floor above us, up on the gallery where a room full of living people, and probably a bunch of ghosts, are watching another person die. Then we hear a voice from up there, diffusing in all the space around us.

Rascal, come up here a minute.

My sister Rosetta. Half-sister, more or less, except I'm adopted and she's not. Chloe's mama. She's got 40 and then some.

I guess they started calling me Rascal because the name they gave me when they took me in is Rasco, after my more or less uncle Rasco who fought the Japs in World War II. That Rasco used to run the projector at the VA hospital, showing movies to the other vets that got their legs blown off or lost their minds somewhere in the war. Some of those hombres, when you would watch them watch those movies, are so far back in that God-forsaken landscape in their heads you couldn't find them with a pack of hounds. I heard Uncle Rasco fought on some islands in the Pacific Ocean. He wouldn't ever talk about the war, and last July 4th he ran his two-tone Ford Sunliner into a whole carload of tourists and got himself and all of them dead. I remember that day especially because it started with Aunt Bug telling me something bad was going to happen because a coyote had killed a black kid, which according to her a self-respecting coyote would rather avoid. I told her coyotes must have a pretty educated palate because I had never noticed a difference between the taste of a black goat and a white one. She said it was no surprise to her that coyotes knew things I didn't. I asked what the bad thing was and she said she wished she knew. Then that night the dogs went nuts and woke us up, and the law stood there on our front porch and told us about the wreck.

Anyway you could see how there could be confusion with two Rascos around, so the one who was late to the party gets to be called Rascal. My old amigo Pepper Hinojosa told me in sixth grade it sounded like a dog's name. *And what does your name sound like?* I asked him, and before either of us could think of an answer I bloodied his nose on principle, but I didn't really care. Most dogs I know beat most people, role model-wise.

I make the stairs complain going up to the landing outside Bug's bedroom and Chloe stays on the sofa. The wood in Bug's house remembers when it was alive in trees, I think, because it vocalizes sometimes, not just when you step on it but in the night when nothing's moving.

Did she die?

No she did not die.

Rosetta's still a pretty woman, Neiman Marcus up and down, black-haired and blue eyed like Daddy, but she's gotten a little heavy and about half mean. It's like some kind of ancient female rage has started seeping through her pores. Sad to contemplate but that's Chloe twenty-some years on, right there. She opens the door and there they all are. Rosetta's dumb ass husband Randal, who runs a Feed and Seed and John Deere dealership with Aunt Bug's money, giving me his best I-know-so-much-you-don't grin from a wingback chair. Old Aunt Dolly in a corner by the window 'cross the room, staring at the closed curtain like she can see right through it. Dolly always reminds me of a wren, those frail little birds that build nests in any shelter they can find around your house. Our Daddy Stafford, still a handsome old cowboy but looking at the downslope and not as tall as he used to be, sits right on the edge of the death bed with one boot on his knee, the pant leg pulled up so you can see the eagle worked into the stitching on the shaft. And the centerpiece of everything is Great Aunt Bug, her visage rising from the pillow like a pale clay model of a hill that hasn't been rained on in a thousand years. Sixty inches down, her feet make two little peaks in the white chenille bedspread. The room is gray as an eclipse. The day is all sealed out.

Did ya'll find somethin' to amuse yourselves? Daddy wants to know.

Not really.

Good.

Her hands are movin', Randal says.

They are. All packed in blotched and peppered rice paper skin, bulged out with swollen bones and rusty tendon wires attached to gnarly claws, Bug's hands are picking in the most tentative way any moving thing has ever picked at the crocheted fringe along the folded portion of the sheet.

Rosetta says *Aunt Bug, honey, can you hear us at all?*

We can't know, Daddy says.

I just want her to know we're here is all.

We can't know what she knows or what she hears.

Well goddamnit Daddy I know we can't, but I can want it can't I?

You can want what you damn well please.

She hears, Randal says. *She can be up here on this mountain and you can't whisper howdy-do in church, all the way in town, without her knowin' it.*

Aunt Bug did lay claim to certain powers. She knew when people were about to die, though she missed on Uncle Rasco. She said that was because he didn't go as a result of a sickness. She knew the big things and the little, and all of it seemed to come to her at random. She knew North Korea would invade South Korea on June 24, 1950. She looked up from breakfast that day and said *Of all the senseless things. Another war just started.* When she was a girl her little brother, our Daddy's Daddy, broke his leg falling down a mine shaft out in the mountains and she dreamed where he was. Without that dream, I suppose, some of us wouldn't be here.

Randal, there are times to talk and times to keep your mouth shut, Rosetta tells him.

We can't know, Daddy says. *She has gone behind the veil.*

Our old Daddy has turned a little mystical on us in his later years. He hasn't started claiming to know things the rest of us didn't, not yet. How Aunt Bug knows is a mystery. I guess the knowing just creeps into her, right through her clothes and skin, or she picks it off the wind or hears it when her house starts talking in the night. Bug claims she inherited this gift of knowing directly from all the Holliday women who came before her. Rosetta says the gift has not been offered to her and that can be the case for all time because she has no use for it. If it's ever cropped up in Chloe she hasn't told me. Maybe Aunt Bug is the end of the line, knowing-wise.

Right then bright light splashes into the room. All of us but Aunt Bug swing and blink. Turns out Aunt Dolly has pulled back the curtain at her window and is tying up the sash. Our heads turn back to Bug to gauge what she will do about all this sunshine pouring through her bedchamber drunk and disorderly without her permission and she does nothing at all. Old Dolly smiles the tiniest baby of a smile and watches a fly worry up against the sun-bright window as though it is the most fascinating spectacle since Creation. She must have heard it buzzing there, and felt a need to see it. She's humming a cheery little tune under the currents of her breath. If she's worried about Bug you sure couldn't tell it. Maybe she figures this whole death thing is just a bump in the road. Or more likely I guess she's tuned in to Dolly radio, as Aunt Bug used to say, on a frequency all her own.

Aunt Dolly don't you think you should close the curtains, sweetheart? Rosetta says. When Rosetta uses that tone of voice it sounds like she wants to pour honey on you, right before she breaks your neck. A beat or two goes by. Then she looks at me and says *We need to think about what we're gonna serve when people come to the house.*

I told you already, Daddy says, *we won't need to serve anything. You know people always bring food.*

And I told you already you know Aunt Bug would want to provide. That's why I called Rascal up here, so he could start cookin' some goat. And I can make my potato salad. Aunt Bug always loved my potato salad.

Randal wiggles his finger so that I will lean down closer.

I didn't know Aunt Bug loved anything but Bombay Gin, he says as quiet as he can manage, but not quiet enough.

Randal, you are truly an idiot, Rosetta says. *Aunt Dolly. Sweetheart. That hummin' is about to drive me batshit crazy.*

Rosetta smooths down her skirt. She crosses to the window, unties the sash, and pulls the curtains to. Aunt Dolly stops humming. Rosetta walks back across the room and gives Randal a look that could shave him.

Light as a mayfly, Dolly opens the curtains, ties up the sash, and picks her tune up where she left it.

I guess ya'll want me to cook some goat I say, and before they can say anything I'm down the stairs. Chloe watches me go past, then gets up and follows me out. The sky is wide open and the wind is picking up. It'll be cold by tonight. I can't tell you why but something sad can happen to a living thing when you put walls around it and a roof between it and the sky. I know I turn more alive when I step outside. In town, they've started building houses that look just alike, in straight rows on a grid of streets that look just alike too. You would get lost in there and never get out except for the street names, which are all the names of birds we never see around here, like Sandpiper and Scarlet Tanager. I wouldn't know a Scarlet Tanager if it built a nest in my hair. When I started to drive—I was around twelve I guess—Aunt Bug asked me to carry her over there so she could see it with her own eyes. That little old woman looked out the window of my Daddy's truck at those rows of new houses like she was on a grand tour of the moon. She pulled her head back in and shook it and *Rascal, I believe we have discovered Birdland* was all she had to say.

If I had to live in one of those houses, I know I'd lift up one fine night crazy as a screech owl and take off down the highway. And if I did, if you or anybody did, you'd fly right past the new country club where they waste water keeping the grass green so Randal and his friends can chase golf balls around. That place has a big paved parking lot and a club house made to look like some jet set villa, with a bar and a restaurant with white linen tablecloths and candles floating in bowls on little boats where the better people of the town can sit and know for damn certain they are the better people, just as good as the better

people in Dallas, with Cadillacs and Lincolns just as big and shiny.
I went to my high school graduation party there and got drunk and
threw up in the swimming pool. I suppose the idea of all those things,
Birdland and the town cut up into squares and the candles in the little
boats, is to give everybody the feeling they're all tame and secure and
tomorrow will be pretty much a replay of today. If you don't need that
feeling you can do fine out here in the mountains.

What's goin' on, Rascal? Chloe says.

We're cookin' goat.

Chloe steps over and gives me a little kiss on the lips which is
strange right out here in the daylight, and we move on and come to the
pen where I keep some young kids with their mothers. Taking care of
them is part of how I earn my keep. That and working cattle, breaking
and training horses, and bringing home a little meat I shoot out on the
range. I don't remember a time I wasn't fooling with the animals some
way on this ranch. They feed us and carry us and pay for everything we
need, and they all take some looking after. Even the goats. You might
think goats are tough. They look it, and in a lot of ways they are. But
when they get the bloat you have to tube them and give them oil and
baking soda to keep them alive, and if you keep Angoras and they get
caught out in heavy rain too soon after they're sheared, they get paralyzed and die real quick. You can lose your whole herd.

When we eat goat on the ranch it's mostly cabrito. The best meat
comes from a Boer kid that weighs maybe ten pounds and has never
had anything in its belly but goat milk. Yeah, you're eating a baby, and
it might be better in a perfect world to let the goat live out its days, but
people like to put that meat in their mouths when it's still tender and
sweet. We separate out one about the right size and Chloe picks it up.
If you plan to kill a living creature the least you can do is look it in
the eye. You need to understand what you're doing, and so does that
creature you're about to kill. In this pen we've got plenty of goats' eyes
to look into, and they're looking right back at us.

The first thing you notice, of course, about a goat's eye is that the pupil is not round like yours, but is a slit that lays out like the horizon. I read in a book that slit gives a goat a field of vision 340 degrees wide, almost all the way around a circle. I don't know how you'd know that for sure without being a goat, but so the book said. You can believe it if you want to, like the Virgin Birth. Or you can try sneaking up on a goat. It's hard to sneak up on anything that is awake and can see in almost all directions without turning its head.

There's no getting around the fact that that eye is spooky, and maybe it's one of the reasons people associate goats with the devil. The devil looks a lot like a goat, in most of the pictures I've seen. There's a bastard of a sticker burr out here people call a goat's head sometimes and a devil's head other times, and it looks like both those things. But a goat is not a devil. Everything mean enough to live in the universe of rock and sand and cactus that falls off in every direction below Aunt Bug's house is designed to make you bleed. Ocotillo, agave, sotol, scorpions, rattlers, big cats, bears, not to mention weather that will fry your ass all day and freeze it all night. Excepting the occasional human, though, none of it is evil. It just doesn't give a damn about you one way or the other.

I know who you are, where you come from, what you want most, the goat's eye says. *And I couldn't care less.*

We take the kid into a barn where I've got a rack for slaughtering. Chloe's petting it, cuddling. I like the way she nuzzles into the fur, smells what's there. It's no compliment if somebody says you smell like a goat, but a goat smells rich in a way no rich man can. I'm of the school that you comfort the animal a while before you kill it. Some say if you don't the adrenaline will toughen up the meat. I don't know if that's true, but it's not why I do it. It just feels right.

I have a long sharp blade I only use for this. You could shave with it if you don't mind risking your neck. I show Chloe how I pin the kid between my legs and pull its head back from behind.

You don't want to hesitate, I say. *Some people shoot 'em or hit 'em in the head first, but a goat's skull is hard and believe it or not that doesn't always work. The cut is the quickest way, and that's what you want.*

I make one clean stroke across the throat just below the jawbone, all the way to the spine.

We tie on some butcher's aprons and wait a minute until we know for sure the kid is dead, then we hang it up head down and drain most of the blood.

I make slits along the underside and around the legs to loosen the skin, cut around the ass and work out a length of intestine, tie it off with twine and cut above the knot.

That's important so you don't contaminate the meat.

Skinning a kid this small is pretty easy.

I cut off the head, gut the goat, and whack it up just like you do a rabbit, break the back in two places, separate it, and take off the legs. A big goat is a different proposition.

Chloe and I repeat the process with three more kids. I do the slaughtering because she doesn't want to try that yet, but she butchers two of them. You can see the concentration in her face, her lips set, her jaw muscle working and her neck tight.

Do I chop the back here?

A little bit lower. I point. *You want to be right below the front legs and right above the back ones.*

She makes a clean cut through with one swing and the carcass jumps from the blow.

Rascal, did Aunt Bug ever say she loved you?

Hell of a question when you're chopping up a goat.

Did she say it to you?

She shakes her head without looking up. Her black hair is shiny, bouncy. Done up with curlers at night I guess.

Old Bug is hard as they come. But she taught me how to do this, just like I'm showing you. Teaching somebody how to live is better than just words.

Could be that's all we're here for, I think, but I don't say it. Chloe's studying the chunks of baby goat she's just laid out with a cleaver and a knife.

We're here to eat each other, the goat's eye says. *That's the best that I can tell.*

A goat will eat anything, and maybe that's why you can't pin down the taste of goat meat to any certain flavor. Cabrito tastes like the open country would if you could roll it all together and roast a piece of it and put it in your mouth, like sex with a little salt and sugar, like knowing where you come from. You have to gnaw to win the last tasty bits from the sharp points of the bone.

Chloe turns around and gives me that little open-mouthed smile. Rosetta invested heavily with the orthodontist, so her teeth are really pretty. We're both all bloody. We wash up in the yellow well water at the basin behind the slaughter rack, then we start working on the pit. There are a lot of ways to cook goat, but on the ranch we like a welded rebar cage buried in a hole in the ground. The meat is falling off the bones when you're done, but it takes all day.

We're stacking wood in the pit when somebody starts yelling up by the house. *Oh my God, oh my God.* We run up there and it's Rosetta, standing out by her Cadillac, Daddy's pickup, and my hunt-rigged Jeep. She's got a hand over her mouth and she's gone white. There's a dust devil dancing like a baby tornado behind her, off at the edge of the mesa.

What's wrong?

Pappy Holliday, she says in this little voice I've never heard her use.

What about him?

Goddamn Pappy Holliday.

Pappy was a one-eyed Indian fighter and Texas Ranger and Aunt Bug's, and Daddy's, and all these people's most distinguished ancestor. He lost the eye in a skirmish when a Comanche warrior shot his horse out from under him and it threw him eyeball-down onto a long mesquite thorn. He used to live in a lean-to not far from where we are now, all decorated with a bunch of skulls and scalps of Comanches, Apaches, and Mexicans he'd killed. The county is named for him. So is the ranch. He died of lockjaw 80-some years ago.

Rosetta, what about him?

Goddamn.

Chloe stays with her and I run on up the stairs. The door to Aunt Bug's room is open. Face down right on the rug in front of me is the dusty bronze bust of Pappy Holliday that sat on top of Bug's armoire as long as anyone remembers. It shows him with the patch that covered up his missing eye. Daddy and Randal are standing there staring at the back of Pappy's head. Aunt Dolly is sitting by her window giggling up a storm. She's trying to stop the giggling by humming at the same time, which appears to be a hard thing. Sounds like she might be doing *Turkey in the Straw.* Aunt Bug's mouth and eyes are open wide. She's looking right through the ceiling. The ruined hill of her face has gone yellow like the water from her pipes.

God Almighty, Randal says, *how can that thing be jumping 'round the room? It must weigh two hundred pounds.*

It was not jumping in this world, Daddy says.

Well, Randal says, *it sure as hell landed in this world. Two inches more that way and it would have broke every bone in my foot.*

Turns out Aunt Bug let loose a death rattle and before anybody could properly notice, Pappy Holliday did a swan dive from the top of his armoire. These things can happen in this part of the world and I guess anywhere. On Uncle Rasco's birthday, a month after the car wreck, all the lights in his house came on in the night, and his girlfriend Esperanza said his old border collie was up whining and wouldn't get quiet.

No use looking because it won't be there in front of you, no matter how wide your field of vision is, but there's something going on that we can't reach out and grab.

One thing we do know is that Aunt Bug has left the ranch. That's hard to imagine because there's never been a time for any of us when she was anyplace else. For Randal and Rosetta, this development probably looks like a color picture of the Promised Land. Ninety-six thousand acres and change without Aunt Bug in the foreground. I guarantee you Randal's been sitting up nights in his plaid Bermuda shorts, wearing pencils to the nub so he can try to multiply the current price per acre of Holliday County land by ninety-six thousand. Or drawing little diagrams of five acre plots he'll sell to Yankees and Californians for twenty times that price. Or dreaming how he'll make water out of dust, irrigate and build a subdivision, a golf club, and an airport for private jets. Of course that means the answer to the secret of the century has to go his and Rosetta's way, and right now Aunt Bug's lawyer Buddy Coleman is the only living human who knows how that tale turns out.

Randal has to figure he's the front-runner in the Aunt Bug rodeo. He and Rosetta have pretty much invested their lives making it that way. Every Sunday in the front pew at First Baptist, where he's a Deacon and she sings solos in the choir. Three legitimate, baptized kids. She's School Board. He's Chamber of Commerce. They watch Ed Sullivan on the biggest television you ever saw. They send out Christmas cards with their pictures on them, where you can count every one of their teeth.

Meanwhile Daddy, the only serious contender left in the field after Uncle Rasco's demise and the only one likely to keep the ranch in one piece, has to figure as a genuine dark horse. Three ex-wives who swear he's Satan, never saw a skirt or a highball or a game of five card stud he didn't like. And then to top it off there's me. I was adopted as a squalling babe after one of Daddy's intimate acquaintances at the time, a lady named Lucinda I never properly met, pushed me through her birth canal and took off with a drummer in a country band. Some claim I am my Daddy's son after all. But nobody really knows, not me or Daddy or anybody else. Whatever you might say about him, and there's a lot you could say, he stood up and took me in, and when he told Aunt Bug about it all she said was *A spotted dog has spotted pups.*

They can put that on my tombstone for all I care.

Aunt Dolly has quit humming. She's working her hands one around the other in her lap. The curtains at her window are closed. Daddy tries to shut Aunt Bug's mouth and eyes, but they keep popping open. He gives her a kiss on the forehead. Rosetta strides in and starts to tidy up. If she's still worried about Pappy Holliday putting his nose through the rug, you can't see it. She pulls the sheet up over Aunt Bug's face. She tells Randal to go out and call the undertaker. Undertaker, now there's a word for all time. Before Randal can make it down the stairs, she yells after him to bring some vaqueros in from the bunkhouse and figure out how to get Pappy back on his perch. *Aunt Dolly*, she says then, all sweet and chirpy, *why don't you go down and make us a nice pot of tea?*

Know what a fulcrum is? Well, Aunt Bug was the fulcrum in this old world, and now she's gone everything will tilt a whole new way. I guess I want to look at things the way I know them one last time. Before Rosetta can think of anything for me to do, I go down the stairs and out to my Jeep. Chloe has wandered over toward the edge of the mesa. She's standing there staring off at the mountains. I pull out my spotting scope and set it up to see if any pronghorns are moving, and find a good bunch off at the base of a peak, maybe two miles out, maybe further. There's a pretty stout mess of wind, dust moving every direction. I tie down the windshield so I can feel it when I drive. I take the .30-06 off the gun mount and throw the bolt back to open the chamber. I know it's clean and well-oiled because I'm the one that cleans it, but I look anyway because that's the right thing to do. The bore is so shiny it would work like a fun house mirror if you could crawl down in it. I've got the scope sighted in at 300 yards, so I won't be looking that prong buck in the eye. He'll never see the bullet coming. He won't have time to think much of anything besides *what the hell*. That's just how it is, because I can't exactly walk up to him and ask his permission. I put the rifle back in the mount. Chloe has come over and wants to go but I tell her she belongs here with her mama, and besides somebody needs to finish the pit.

Who do you belong with? she says. I fire up the Jeep.

I look into her face before I pull away and know it's one of those pictures I will see forever, as long as I have eyes to close and memories.

There used to be an ocean out here, volcanoes and flying dinosaurs and mountains of ice and people decked out in paint and feathers dancing up in the caves. I'm not sure all of that is gone, completely, though it is invisible, at least for me. Maybe old billy goat can see it. I know there is something that will chill your blood down in the evening, when it moves just outside the little circus ring of things you can perceive. Soon enough this old world will be there too. You can already see its bones. It's finished, and there will be a new world walking on its grave. You can feel that world's impatience. It can't wait. It'll be air-conditioned, and paved, and all quiz shows and deodorant. That much you can tell already.

I've got up a pretty good head of steam now, bouncing like a wild-cat down the old ranch road and eating sand when I open my mouth to give out a grito. Maybe I'll bring back a buck and maybe I won't. Maybe I'll just keep going.

Smash and Grab

I came here as an honest tradesman. *Here* is a curbside opposite ten thousand square feet of faux palazzo on a hilltop, overlooking a vast lake with distant sails filling in the warm air of morning and a toy skyline made of temples of commerce at the last edge of the vista. The façade is painted Greek fishing village white, the roof is terra cotta, with a loggia peaking the roofline like an unfortunate hat. In the foreground, a nymphless fountain tosses a fat plume of water skyward. Side arches lead down rock work paths to a series of courtyards and to the zero edge pool in the rear with its spa of native limestone and its bubbling urns.

No doubt all of this adds value on the property tax rolls, but for yours truly the home's greatest attractions are its contents and its perfect isolation. The contents are yet to be revealed, but if my intelligence is right they include an exquisite if small collection of ancient Hindu artifacts. The isolation is apparent. The hilltop lot, acres big, is separated from the nearest structure by a sharply spiraling road. No neighbor can see the house without hopping in the Bentley or committing to a strenuous hike. In the course of observation, via binoculars, from a nearby hillside, I have established that the occupants—an Indian whose company develops software, his willowy trophy of a wife, and their two small children—are out well before 8am on weekdays, that the cleaning crew comes Mondays and Thursdays, the landscapers every other Wednesday, and the pool man on Friday. I note now that there are no vehicles parked outside the house and no obvious activity.

I take the parabolic listening device from its place in my equipment bag, cover my ears with the headphones and switch on the power. I point the microphone and its black dish toward the front wall of the house. The brand name of this tool delights me. *The Bionic Ear.* I bought it on the internet. A fancy toy, but listening technology is nothing new.

You may recall that in Polybius' account of the Roman siege of Ambracia, for example, the defenses of the city's inhabitants were so effective that the legions under the command of the consul Marcus Fulvius Nobilior had to resort to digging a mine under the walls. After a time the people inside noticed a suspicious pile of dirt and debris outside their battlements, growing ever larger. They did some digging of their own, fashioning a deep trench parallel to the wall, and along the wall-side of this trench they placed a row of very thin implements made of brass. Sound vibrating through the brass soon gave them the exact location of the Roman tunnel and they dug a countermine to surprise the invaders. Fulvius eventually made it through anyway, despoiling the city of everything of value, including the cult images from its temples. Livy tells us the Ambracians later complained to the Roman Senate that they were reduced to the worship of bare walls and doorposts. But that is another story. My point is that The Bionic Ear is my brass implement.

What my implement mostly detects is the loud churr of the fountain. I avoid it as best I can, scanning walls methodically, then go back for a random sampling at specific points. But even the Ambracians could hear nothing worthwhile from this position. I am forced to abandon my van with a bulky microphone in my hands and earphones on my head. My new angle from the side of the house, under the cover of a tall juniper, greatly improves my reception. I hear the purr of an air conditioning system, its breath untroubled. No doubt the filters are changed out monthly by a service, so the inhabitants never suffer from stuffy noses or soiled hands. But I am listening for what I do not hear. No television. No music. No quarrels or love making or gossip on a phone. No vacuum cleaner piloted by the hand of a maid. I risk a complete circuit of the house, eavesdropping from the back and the opposite side. Nothing. I return to the van and replace the Ear in its bag, extract and snap on a pair of latex gloves, ready to operate.

Strangely empowered by my rubber hands, I pick up more equipment. My *Stinger* all-steel battering ram, likewise purchased on the internet, is almost three feet long but weighs only thirty-five pounds. Like the SWAT units and firefighters who employ it, I enjoy this device because a couple of good swings with it will splinter most doors.

My bee keeper's hat and veil is gear I consider an innovation. The hat is a pith helmet. The veil, a coated black steel screen, hangs on a frame of plastic bars. It affords an ideal combination of visibility and invisibility: I see out, the security cameras do not see in. The effect is comical, I admit, but I am dressed for work, not for a cocktail party.

With the hat on my head, the Stinger in one hand and two duffel bags enclosing a supply of bubble wrap for the protection of precious objects in the other, I check the empty road, step down from the vehicle and move toward the front walk as though I belong there. I pass a placard on a stick, advising that the house is protected by ADT Security. I have my own brand name to announce. A magnetic sign attached to the door of my nondescript white van says *Swift Chimney Sweeps,* and provides a URL for a web site that is so virtual it does not exist. I never use the same sign twice. I am CEO of an empire of imaginary businesses. Today my company dress code consists of a khaki-colored poplin short-sleeve coverall of the generic variety favored by workmen everywhere. A name tag sewn onto the breast pocket says *Felix.*

That may as well serve as my name. One lifetime ago I wore another name, that of Pliny Jarrings. Pliny's bona fides were these: Doctor of Philosophy, Churchill College, Cambridge; PhD Classics, Harvard; MA Art History, University of Fribourg; employment at demise as Eliza F. Philburn Distinguished Professor of Philosophy and Classics at a tax-supported university more noted for its football team than its philosophers. Pliny was the author of eight books including an authoritative guide to Wittgenstein (complimented by its most perceptive critic as *notoriously difficult*) and two slender volumes of poetry. Pleased to offer you his acquaintance, and may he rest in peace.

I mount the steps, cross the broad stained concrete porch and admire the heavy brass knocker in the center of the door, a woman's hand grasping a globe. The detail is remarkable. It is the hand of a Devi, alive, delicate, and strong. She wears two rings. I take the hand in mine and let it drop. A dense sheet of sound waves through the house. The sound is impressive. I make it again. I waste a minute wondering how long it might take to remove the knocker and put in my bag. I push a lighted button beside the door, generating a conventional, lazy ding-dong from inside. Ding-dong again. No one to welcome me. No obvious video installation though no doubt my every move is recorded and perhaps displayed on distant screens. The thought inspires some urgency. I put down the duffels and take the Stinger in both hands, eyeing a point near the lock. But before I swing—why not?—I let go with one hand and try the knob, an oversized affair that fits in my latex palm like a softball. The door opens with an eerie, silent glide.

I face a hallway with portals on three sides, a staircase to the upper reaches, a feeling of unlimited space. I hear not a sound. The floor is creamy, polished stone, the walls a mossy green. Directly ahead of me, as the guardian of the entrance, stands a four foot tall stone linga with Shiva's face on its business end, bearing the third eye of supreme wisdom. A small, chrome-finished spotlight graces the countenance of the god. I wonder briefly about the mindset of a homeowner who greets guests just in the door with an ancient super-sized dildo. And then I wonder how I will ever cart it off. I have a dolly in the van, but I am not eager to pay for the object with a hernia. I set that consideration aside for the moment, put the Stinger down on the porch and take up the duffels.

The unlocked door has spooked me, I admit. Still the house beckons. It is an undiscovered territory, a frontier of potential. But as Wittgenstein said of language, it may be just as well *an immense network of easily accessible wrong turnings.* I spot motion detectors but no alarm has sounded. There must be cameras but they are well concealed. I step to the security console and learn from its display that the system is switched off. Why would that be? Fulvius would go forward, but then he had Rome behind him. Pliny would retreat. I will not. I march across the opening into a vast *living area,* confected to inspire humility in the plebian mortal, with seating pods floating in a sea of open space and a glass wall overlooking the pool and the domain of hills. A trapezoid of filtered sunlight paints the cold floor. The furniture mingles antique South Asian and toneless modern, the present mashed up with the past. But the art is stunning.

The space cannot decide if it is a home or a museum. It does know it is not a temple. I whiff no incense. See no evidence of red kumkum powder, no yellow nuggets of turmeric, garlands of flowers or bits of broken coconut. The self-conscious, spotlit displays make it clear these are not *murti,* not images to channel gods. They are possessions, here to signify the peacock demigod who owns them. Through the fine mesh of my veil, I admire each piece briefly in its turn, ever conscious that I must make my choices quickly. An excellent seated Ganesha, of ivory, about eight inches high. Fifteenth century or so. A stone head of Krishna, perhaps the oldest work in the collection.

And now a spellbinding representation of the goddess Durga slaying the demon Mahisha, 12th century, carved in yellow-beige stone and standing about six inches tall. This object is familiar because it was featured in an article I found about the house and its owner. Durga is missing one of her hands, reportedly one that held a spear, but she is well provided with weaponry. Various of the rest of her sixteen hands hold an arrow, sword, chisel, hammer, thunderbolt, elephant goad, war discus, shield, bow, bell, mirror, and a noose. For the battle, Mahisha has taken the form of a buffalo. Inadequate cover, as it turns out, for Durga has whacked off the buffalo's head. The demon emerges from the decapitated body in the form of a small fat man with a necklace of snakes. He looks up at his killer admiringly, even as her pet lion nibbles his toes.

Touring this gallery, I sense as I so often do in my work the adhesive, mocking quality of the objects. They watch me as intensely as I view them. They crave and despise my attention. To fully exist, we require one another, but neither of us is happy with the arrangement. I am happy, however, with the quality and quantity of all I see in the downstairs of the house alone. I can afford to be selective.

The stairs ascend in a graceful curve, carpeted in a red floral-patterned runner of Rajasthani silk that muffles the sound of my footsteps. In fact, as I climb, the silence of the house grows deeper, thicker. I stop cold at the last bend, for on the edge of the landing I can just now see, dangling from the top step with a weightless gravity, is a human hand.

A shape shifter is one who can inhabit the body of a new kind of being. Witches do it, we are told, but no supernatural training is required. With effort and commitment, one can stride out of one life into another. But just as the witch remains the witch in the shuck of the crow or the coyote, indelible traces of the old life remain. And in fact the central problem of the new life is that every second living it creates its own gummy complications. There is no zero moment to which one may return or in which one may take shelter.

Would I make the leap again? No doubt. Or better, no choice. In that past life, Pliny woke exhausted by the prospect of his commitments, the foremost being to live through the entirety of another day as Pliny himself. He knew the need to change with the desperation of a passenger on a ship with its bow sucking ocean. It was not an impulse. Not a stab at self-improvement. It was a mandate from the living core that is unburdened by a name, a non-negotiable directive to transmogrify.

He gathered the will to rise from his bed, sewn into his ways as surely as if he faced the world in a woolen overcoat lined with scrap iron. He descended an accustomed flight of stairs, clutching at the banister with cold, damp palms, into an accustomed kitchen, where he kindled the same burner on the same stove and set the same kettle with its spout always pointing east.

He had lived in the same apartment for thirty years, walked the same sidewalks and eaten the same meals in the same restaurants. Dozed through the same conferences and fought the same oh-so-academic skirmishes. It is true that he once loved teaching—the living discourse with minds not yet fixed in cement—had all the awards and top ratings on the campus web sites, but even that went stale in time. The day came when he looked out across his lecture hall onto pod-like, social media-infested batches of young twerps. (Unfair, untrue, says the ghost of Pliny from the cellarage. There were still those faces in the mass upturned toward him full of trust and eagerness to learn that was absolute and pure. But there was nothing left in Pliny grand enough to rise in answer, and the failure in that cut him deeply.)

To be clear, it wasn't death he contemplated. That option presented the unacceptable possibility of eternity—of living on forever in a sanitized version of the suburbs, with playscapes, weenie roasts, and gospel sing-a-longs. Or reincarnation, little better, featuring recycled Pliny looking out the port holes of a tapeworm or riding the tender pocket of a marsupial, eager to dance and gleam again in the light of the world.

No. Pliny was simply through being Pliny, done with his own exhausted tread down his own ever-deepening ruts.

The question came early and often: was such change possible? At first he did not know. He resolved to begin by changing what he could. Changing the outside, he reasoned, must have some effect upon the inside. The one variable in Pliny's life had been his lovers. They had come and gone, but the changes in the guard had always been effected by them, never by him. This time it would be different. He would extricate himself from the clammy web of his relationship with Claire Baker, the wife of his department chairperson. Then he would resign his post, then disappear, one thing before another in sequence, as notes ordered on a scale.

Pliny mounted his bicycle and set out across the bridge that connected his neighborhood to the central city. His first stop would be the museum where Claire spent Wednesday afternoons as a docent. The river winked at him tirelessly with its gray chop. The sun was in hiding. Nothing shined. A light rain began to fall. It occurred to him that this could be the occasion when the bridge collapsed, and he patted the handlebars of the bike, thanking it for fifty thousand times across, fifty thousand times back home. His gratitude, he reasoned, should be good for something in keeping his bicycling form suspended above the water for a few more seconds. He marveled again, as he did often, at the powerful resource his fellow humans made of denial. Everyone above the age of reason and spared dementia knew certainly that a bridge would collapse, an airliner plummet from the sky, and the seed of a fatal disease sprout like a demented joke told deep in the house of the body on the most beautiful day in the world. And yet he was surrounded by commuters happy as embryos in the eggshells of their accelerating cars.

He arrived at the museum, left his bike unlocked—another change—charged up the stairs and through the halls and approached Claire from behind as she led a covey of Sun City seniors just off the tour bus through the Impressionist wing. Against his own better judg-ment he admired the long, fine turn of her calves arising from black high heels and the taut sphere of her exercised bottom as displayed by her sensibly docentesque black skirt. She wore the apricot silk blouse that did so much for her color, unfastened at the neck and revealing downward the promising sliver of flesh that ended in a seam just above the heart, a glimpse of surface territory Pliny knew would go from pearl to deepest rose when there was passion or laughter or humiliation within. He realized how covert and dangerous this knowledge was, how invincible a tar baby the very thought of it might be. He tried seeing Claire as an abstraction, an image made of dots and streaks on a canvas. But as he rounded the troop of seniors and stood facing her from behind their last rank his heart betrayed him and ran like a long shot at the Derby.

Claire made eye contact and acknowledged his presence with an eyebrow. She finished speaking about Matisse's *Woman Reading in a Garden.* She asked for questions. Pliny raised his hand.

How can I tell you I can't see you anymore? he asked. It was a genuine question, Wittgensteinian in nature, touching on the potent inadequa-cy of language.

The seniors turned as one. The woman nearest Pliny moved her reading glasses up her nose to better study his profile. He watched Claire gather herself. She was not close enough for him to enjoy the full effect, but he knew the color was on the rise behind the silk, up the sharp V of fragrant, kindling skin.

Go away, Pliny, she said.

He did as he was told.

Next, he awaited Julius M. Baker, Doctor of Philosophy, Yale, Quinien quibbler, satrap for the mindless moneyed, in the chairman's prim, anally constricted office. Baker never appeared. Doubtless he was held by a more imperative appointment. Pliny left him a signed note on a pad with Baker's name and credentials printed at the top. *I resign from the faculty,* it said. And then *Regards to Claire,* with a smiley face beneath. Drawing it, he pondered briefly on what the *Lectures and Conversations on Aesthetics, Psychology, and Religious Belief* might imply about Wittgenstein's potential views on emoticons. The thought led nowhere. He felt an enormous relief.

As Pliny pedaled away from campus, the lights of the oncoming cars beamed ahead in the rain like promise itself.

But what would he do with his time in this new life, if he was no longer to publish philosophical tracts and teach pup philosophers to fetch? His education and experience did not suggest a career path outside academia. He was a bit long in the tooth to re-train. And earning a paycheck as a datapoint among the cogs of an incorporated entity did not appeal.

The swift delivery of his answer came as a surprise. While he pushed a cart between the bright rows of brands in the detergent aisle at the supermarket, an unknown individual penetrated the locked door of his new apartment, apparently with the aid of a crowbar, and freed him from his laptop computer. Far from feeling victimized, he was inspired so completely that he dropped dead on the spot and, after the briefest transmigration, I emerged from his ashes, bold as Fulvius on his charger, into the brilliance of that particularly cloud-free afternoon.

Plunder was so obvious a solution! It was time-honored, the world's second oldest profession at a minimum. From an ethical standpoint, it was near blameless, as my own mission statement would be to take only from those who could afford the benefit of being taken from. They were consummate consumers, after all. My debits from their possessions would provide them the opportunity to do what they enjoy most: acquire more things. They would not wish to appear vulnerable among their peers and, worse, among the proletarian throng, and thus might be hesitant to publicly report their losses. Pliny's training in and enthusiasm for antiquities and art would serve me well in my new calling. And as a practical matter, this strategy would assure a high return on my investments of time and energy, because the proceeds would be precious in the eyes of the world. In terms of the competitive landscape I would be, as far as I could tell, sui generis among the common practitioners, such as my role model, who smashed and grabbed at every random opportunity to keep a drug of choice thrilling through their arteries.

In a moving ceremony, Pliny's impressively framed diplomas, once displayed like hunting trophies, were consigned to a bonfire. I observed, admiring the dancing figures in the flames, how documents that purport to confer identity can in fact conceal it. I was so much more the new being than the old.

I invested six months in the study of the literature of my chosen trade. There are few how-to manuals and post-graduate courses on burglary, aside from those available within the walls of prisons. But there are abundant texts on the prevention of burglary and the apprehension of burglars, on theft-defeating devices and the like. It was a pedestrian exercise to turn this fearful knowledge on its head. I took more pleasure in the chronicles of those I wished to join as a peer in the craft.

Flaubert, for instance, in his first published story—*Bibliomania*—drew upon this fertile history. The story steals the case of Don Vicente, a Spanish monk who began his career with the simple pilfering of rare tomes from his monastery's library. In 1830, Vicente dropped out of the order and set up shop in Barcelona as a seller of antiquarian books. He improved his stock by plundering other booksellers, with a passion so rabid that he murdered his rivals and removed their best stuff before burning down their homes and places of business. His downfall was that he could not bear to part with his favorite acquisitions. I understand this failing all too well. At his trial he explained his philosophy. *Every man must die, sooner or later,* he said, *but good books must be conserved.* A noble sentiment, even if I found little in the monk's methodology to incorporate into my practice.

As the next step in my plan of action, I cemented a relationship with an associate known in the parlance as a *fence.* The late, un-lamented Pliny had hoisted a few tumblers of ouzo in the University Club with one Teddy Diomidis, a darkly curl-topped bear of a dealer in antiquities known for his skill in redistributing bell kraters, Etruscan spear tips, statuary, and other items encrusted with cultural patina from their countries of origin to museums and private owners. In his cups, Teddy liked quoting Heraclitus, and he saw Pliny as a useful companion due to his ability to throw quotes back across the table.

No man ever steps in the same river twice, he would say.

And Pliny would answer *Ah so, but the literal translation is so much more elusive. It runs more like this: In the same river we both step and do not step, we are and are not. And only then does brother Heraclitus tell us: It is not possible to step twice into the same river.*

And Teddy, undaunted, with loads of smiling charm, would offer *The path up and down is one and the same.*

I knew that discretion was the essence of Teddy's profession. I confided the bones of my business model to him and he confirmed that, were I to deliver items of value, he would present them for sale to his clients in return for a generous commission.

The rest was common sense. Following Heraclitus' good example, I taught myself by questioning myself, and my first operations were seamless—and quite profitable—ventures. The proceeds ran into the millions. In fact I discovered that the most time-consuming aspect of my reeducation was learning how to hide the money. Teddy's counsel was most useful in that regard. I did acquire a few gadgets I thought might help me along, but nothing about breaking and entering is rocket science.

———

The fingers of the hand, though thick, curve gracefully. I take the last four steps with some deliberation. I do not move past the edge of the landing. The body is a middle aged man's. The head is bald. It rests on its right side, eyes wide, mouth gaping, in a slick of inspissated blood that blots out the flowers on the carpet. The most outstanding feature of the head is the ordinary, household claw hammer driven claws first into the back of its pate. The effect is that the head came with a handle attached, by which it could be waggled about. I do not put this to the test. I recognize the head as that of the paterfamilias of the household. I have watched him leave for work on several occasions from my vantage point on the adjoining hill. This is the former Natarajan Mehta, a software magnate whose company fashions brains for the computers of the financial services industry, with a global sales force and a sprawling campus of developers in Bangalore. The cracked shell of Mr. Mehta is dressed casually. His belly spills out beneath a golf shirt that has come untucked from his slacks. He wears slippers.

I descend the stairs in double time. As I round the bend in the staircase I see two beefy Sheriff's deputies, one he, one she, blocking the open doorway below. My Stinger battering ram rests just outside the door. I have a veiled bee keeper's hat on my head and two empty duffel bags in my hands, which are sealed in surgeon's gloves. I am not the picture of innocence. Schopenhauer said *The world is my idea*. He was wrong.

Socrates was surrounded by his students as he waited in his cell for the hemlock to kick in, and he took advantage of the teaching moment to explain how irrational it is to fear something we know nothing about, i.e., death. My cell mate in the county lockup is a cadaverous old man with an insinuating, tooth-deprived smile. He smells of rotted meat. He amuses himself with mumbles in the language Wittgenstein identified as Privatish, a self-invented tongue only he can understand. In an interlude of silence, his jaundiced eye falls in my direction and he appears to notice me for the first time. I decide to try a little Socrates.

Does the soul admit of death? I ask him.

He endangers himself with laughter, ending a long spasm in wheezes and violent coughs that bend his slight body in half. The air that reaches us through the bars jumps with curses, screams, metallic slams. There seems little opportunity to teach.

But at that moment a guard materializes at the iron portal with a visitor, a lawyer referred by Teddy Diomidis, who wears a hand-tailored suit, a salty goatee, and an oily ducktail haircut.

He brings welcome news. The late Mr. Mehta's widow, together with her children, has been apprehended at a customs desk in Mumbai, and has confessed to wielding the hammer. She is more Durga than willowy trophy, it appears. I remain on the hook, the lawyer tells me, on a variety of charges, and the District Attorney is staying up nights devising more. Even so, my astute counsel points out with a conspiratorial bounce of eyebrows, since I didn't have time to steal anything and didn't even break the door, the worst my captors can make stick at the moment is criminal trespass. He will arrange my bail. Before we part company, he pulls me toward him and whispers with the hairs of his goatee against my ear. In the unlikely chance that I might have committed similar offenses dressed in a beekeeper's bonnet and swinging a battering ram, he says, it is just possible that my modus operandi might lead an interested party to a review of the aforesaid priors, some of which may possibly have involved major acquisitions from persons in a position to throw weight if not money around in the legal system, i.e., people who pay to have judges elected and prosecutors employed. He pulls away and delivers a look that underscores his meaning. Red tracers run through his eyes.

Late the next afternoon I meet Teddy over espresso at a sidewalk café I have never visited before. The light dances around us. Birds eavesdrop in the tree overhead. The eyes of the waitress reflect the deepening colors of the sky. It has never been more clear that everything is sentient, that the very stones are frozen music, as Pythagoras observed. Teddy is ebullient. He reminisces about his boyhood on an island his family owns in the Aegean. It is a paradise for gentlemen and scholars, he tells me, a place a man of my caliber, for example, would be both welcome and invisible, in return for a negotiable fee. He leans back to regard the sunset, overtaken by a philosophic cast.

The sun is new each day, he says.

Change alone is unchanging, I answer.

The Comfort Zone

I have a shirt that sings. There is nothing else extraordinary about it, it's a simple cotton tee. If you care to know what it looks like, there is a crimson silhouette of a leaping dog, a Golden Retriever kind of dog with a Frisbee in its jaws, screen-printed on a field of periwinkle blue. The shirt only knows one song, and sings it in the voice of Annie Lennox:

> *You didn't stand by me*
> *No not at all*
> *You didn't stand by me*
> *Noooo way*

The tune is catchy, and I confess that no matter how I resist it, it often sets my body swaying and my neck bouncing to the rhythm. This can be maddening, because the shirt only knows the chorus of its only song. And because I happen to play Mozart, Beethoven, and Brahms for a living. I'm not, I assure you, a musical snob, but if I'm going to listen to a shirt sing I'd prefer a tune more in line with my own tastes.

The first time the shirt sang I was driving. I jumped and almost lost control. At first I thought the radio had come on without my touching the power button. The windshield wipers do this on occasion but not the radio, so I was a bit unnerved until I realized it was the shirt that was singing.

That made perfect sense. There was no mystery over where the shirt had learned its snatch of song. A woman I betrayed played it on a boom box over and over as I cleared out my possessions from her apartment. Why do I say *a woman* as if she had no name? She has a name. It is Collette. Collette is a perfectly admirable woman, lovely in every way, generous and kind, with large, gold-flecked brown eyes, classically sculpted cheekbones, and a pixie haircut. She is a well-regarded painter best known for her portraits of women with their hair on fire. This very real person with a name, Collette, whom I betrayed, played the song over and over on a boom box as I cleared out my possessions. The boom box sat on the hardwood floor of her dining room, and Collette sat on a straight back wooden chair drinking brandy from a snifter and leaning over to restart the song each time it came to an end.

I was leaving on a tour, and the woman I was taking with me was not Collette.

I don't know why I should be surprised. That's your pattern, isn't it, Louis? She said as she bent to push the button on the boom box. *One woman per world tour?*

She was on target, of course, and as my companion on the previous tour she knew it. The inanity of my behavior as a serial monogamist, packaged and presented with a pop song and the odor of good brandy, made me numb. I am an anachronism as dated as the music I play. That's what she wanted me to hear.

There are many ways to play a single piece of music. People like to hear music the way they are accustomed to it, the way they heard it on a recording that was important to them or at a concert they may have attended or may be able to play back on a screen. My popularity as a performer, such as it is, depends to some extent on my fealty to reproduction of the familiar. The comfort zone, it's called. I live my life there, perhaps as most beings do. Inevitably, it is a life of patterns.

The shirt, I should mention, has a connection with Collette. She bought it and gave it to me when we were traveling in Seattle, just because I had admired it in a store. After that she washed and folded it, over and over, and placed it in the proper order in the drawer she had organized for my tee shirts, just as she maintained other drawers and closets for the rest of my possessions.

I know what you're thinking. If I don't like the shirt's choice of songs, why don't I throw it away, or pass it on to St. Vincent De Paul? Or perhaps I could bring in a *houngan* or an exorcist to recast a silence in the cloth. I don't do any of that because I know it's not that simple. I understand the power at the heart of things.

I'm guessing you do too. Don't you have shoes that have been to too many funerals, and don't they stink of tuberoses?

I once picked up a stone I fancied on the shore in Scotland. It is coal black and the size and shape of an index finger. I felt a twinge as I put it in my pocket, a clear sense of anxiety coming from the stone, a signal that it wanted to stay where it was. I dismissed this as a foolish notion, but I was wrong. Now the stone moves of its own volition around my apartment, appearing on a windowsill or the computer keyboard or, most dramatically, on the hard milk surface of the sink. Sometimes I think I hear it keening in the night.

There is a terrible beauty about such things that has been with me all my life. Early in my career as a schoolboy, the teacher passed out bars of Ivory soap and little paring knives and told us to make the soap into anything we pleased. A blameless creative exercise. The wonder is we didn't whack off our fingers or cut each other's throats. The other children went to work and produced lumpy rabbit heads, cartoon cars, and humanoids that looked like juju dolls. I remember these things as lovely little works of primitive art, and how I envied my classmates their innocence. But I felt the existence of the soap in my hand and knew the deformity and pain that would result if I cut into it. The teacher sent me home with a note that said *Louis won't cut soap*.

In my first memory I'm under the ledge of the keyboard on the upright piano in my parents' living room, too small to climb up on the stool, with my legs splayed out around some wooden blocks. They say I cried if they moved me from that spot, and that the first time someone held me on the stool I made music with the keys. It was my mother, all her sins be forgiven, who realized the only thing to do was give me lessons.

At five I was playing *Für Elise* when my hands and the piano first gave up their separation and produced a sound that reached into my soul and took me prisoner. You can call me crazy, it's not like no one else has, or say that it's impossible, but I went cold all through. I struck the C major chord and held it, sat on that swiveling stool with the up and down screw extended to its highest point beneath me and wept like a man who had been to war.

The Latin root of *prodigy*, I understand, can mean unnatural, a monster.

My awareness would cost me. I grew lanky and exposed, upward but not outward, like a malnourished weed. My head stuck up above the other children, so that I was always looking at their hair. I refused to play football and baseball with the other boys. I suffered cruel taunts and the attacks of bullies. My parents fretted, particularly my father. Normalizing influences were sought. A pal of my father's suggested the Boy Scouts. This would toughen me, the pal said, make me ready for the world. My father was delighted to learn that the Scoutmaster doubled as a boxing coach, and organized boxing tournaments for the troop.

I knew, of course, that I was more than *ready for the world*, just not the world my father had in mind. I had already taken firsts in several competitions. I fought with all I had as he dragged me screaming to my first Scout meeting.

There was not a good fit between the Scouts and me. When the time came for my first boxing match, I entered the ring with my long arms drooping at my sides. I was afraid for my fingers. My opponent, a full head shorter, charged like an apprentice bull and began pummeling my narrow abdomen. All I could see of him was his burr haircut.

Put up your hands! the Scoutmaster shouted.

I didn't want to put up my hands, because I knew the little bull would hit them. Then I had an inspiration. I realized the advantage of my reach, laid a boxing glove flat on the haircut in front of me and straight-armed the boy so that all he could do was punch the air.

Don't just hold him off. Hit him! Hit him!

But I didn't. I kept up my tactic until I heard the bell ring. The Scoutmaster's face was florid and disfigured. He looked like he'd been boxing. He was not unhappy when I was allowed to quit the Scouts.

I did learn something of interest from the Boy Scout Manual, though. I learned Morse Code. The very first example the manual offered of the code was SOS. My father told me (I later learned he was wrong) this stood for *Save Our Souls.* Not Save Our Bodies or Save Our Bacon but Save Our Souls. It seemed to me the most urgent message in the world.

I tapped the message on my desk at school with a pencil until the teacher made me stop, beat it on the lid of a garbage can with a wooden dowel, sent it in middle C from the piano keyboard. One night I stood at a rear window of my home with my Boy Scout signal flashlight beaming SOS into the night. Short short short long long long short short short over and again until my thumb gave out. I believed no one had seen the signal, knew with a final and desolate certainty that no one would ever respond, even if I could signal SOS without stopping for the remainder of my days.

But a neighbor named Mrs. McClung did see the light beaming directly in her kitchen window, which faced the rear of our home across a patch of struggling Bermuda grass. She called the police.

I remember three quick knocks that sent an authoritative echo through the house. I stood at my father's elbow looking through the screen door at a fat policeman with a face like the man in the moon.

Mrs. McClung says someone in your house is shining a flashlight through her window.

Someone in my house. Louis, have you been shining lights?

No sir.

My father taught English at the Junior High. He was a small, bald-headed, precise man who specialized in intimidation. He gave the policeman the look he used on failed spellers, and spoke in a withering tone.

No one in my house is shining lights at Mrs. McClung.

The policeman looked disappointed. He threw a knowing glance at me, apologized to my father and made the porch creak as he turned to go. I hid the flashlight under my mattress.

Shortly afterwards I fell in love for the first time. The focus of my affections was a girl my age, Mary Catherine, who lived directly across the street. Mary Catherine's proximity was the glory and the agony of my days. After school I stood at the window, the piano abandoned at my back, and stared at her front door, the moment when the door would swing open and she would appear advancing in my imagination like the Hindenburg. As she skipped rope on her front sidewalk my heart skipped too—stupidly, traitorously, sloshing in a bog of pain. I wished with an honest and pathetically conflicted passion that Mary Catherine's family would move away, not across town but across the world, so that I would never be tempted to watch her skip again.

One day my mother set out to make an evangelizing call upon the house across the street, on behalf of the church where I spent Sundays in scratchy, stifling clothes. Because the piano was in the living room, and because I spent hours there each day at practice, the room had become my special domain. Violating my space while I stood watch at the window, my mother announced that I should come along with her as an apprentice evangelist.

They're Catholics! I whined.

All the more reason, dear, my mother said.

I said I had to practice. She said *Practice is a pastime. This is the Lord's work.* A pastime? I stamped and tantrumed as I hadn't done since my last trip to a Scout meeting. In the end she clamped her hands on both my wrists and pulled me across the street as if I were a balking mule. My downcast tear-dripping eyes watched the boards of a periwinkle porch go by. My mother let go with one hand and knocked with the other. The door came open, revealing Mary Catherine. I realized with horror that she looked exactly like a chipmunk with freckles, an upturned nose, and eyes the color of her front porch. My heart jumped rope.

Mary Catherine's mother invited us in. My mother settled in a wingback chair and began the conversation chirpingly, as though she had never pulled anyone across any street at any time. Avoiding Mary Catherine's blue gaze, I focused on an object that stood alone on the family mantel. It was a small silver globe on three pod-like, curving legs. It was antique and tarnished but something in it glimmered at me and drew me across the room. I took it in my hands for close examination. With awe I realized the bit of filigree along its circumference could be a kind of handle. I gave the handle a lift with my finger and the top half of the orb flew back. Inside was a perfect cavity, smooth, lustrous, and empty. Whatever its function might have been, I knew it was a female object. I climbed inside and pulled the lid shut behind me. The space was familiar. I recognized it as the orb of my music, my sanctuary from all mundanity, entanglement, and consequence. I could hear a suggestion of polite conversation through the silver wall.

According to my therapist, it is no surprise that this experience is associated with the trial of my first infatuation. Its lesson has served throughout my life. When pressed while unarmed with a piano, I revisit Mary Catharine's front room and seal myself away into a space no unpleasantness can penetrate, an orb of ideal acoustics.

Clearly it was need for armored shelter as much as love of music that spurred me to the labor that would build my rarified life. And believe me it was labor. Much as I loved it, I worked like the devil for it. By my early teens, the firsts I scored were coming in international competitions. At fifteen I played Tchaikovsky's piano concerto with the Chicago Symphony, standing in for Stefan Glockheim, who suffered from an ulcerated stomach. The performance was a triumph. From that day all I would have to do, ever, was more of what I lived for. My travels and studies transported me to an exile I welcomed from my parents and their town. Before you judge, know that I do not lack empathy for them or for all they represent of an unassuming, duty-bound life. I never asked to be a prodigy, and they never asked to raise one. But distance was peace and perspective.

When the time came I discovered the bodies of women only because I had first discovered the hold the music gave me over them. It didn't just gain entrée to bedrooms, it spread the door wide. And a good thing, too. Without the music, I would not have made much progress in the sexual direction. I was and am shy, offbeat, and gawking, all hands and feet and elbows. Maybe my narrow shoulders do support a head classic enough in its proportions to be considered handsome and maybe I can spin a line of conversation when required. I can hold my own in an affair of love, for a time. It is only when the air of the bedroom becomes too close that I begin to have my problems. Always the prodigious monster shows his face. Always the misfit boy is leaving home again.

The end result, as Collette observed, is a career in romance that neatly parallels the career at the keyboard, one woman per world tour.

But what women they have been! Janice, the flame-haired psycho-analyst who changed the locks to our love nest while I was at the store. Yolanda, the doe-eyed potter, who chunked prize-winning vases like Sandy Koufax. The delicate Sumiko, the oboist, who took wire cutters to the strings in my practice room. They all had their reasons.

Measured by women or concerts, the years flew by. Perhaps, I'll admit, I might have made better use of the time. But understand: my hands are mere extensions of the keys. It is not a partnership, it is an entity. My hours in the safe harbor of that entity are the only times I really know who I am and where I'm going. Anachronism that I may be, I am an instrument, and instruments are good for certain things and not for others.

By the time I turned fifty, my insulation from the world came near perfection. For business affairs, I had a manager. I was surrounded by accountants, lawyers, organizers, travel consultants, yogins, and housekeepers in the way warlords are surrounded by elite troops. It likely goes without saying that the center point of this support group was my woman of the moment, the provider not only of cleaned and folded shirts but of harmony and meaning.

At this point, after Colette and after the woman after Colette, I stood apart from my accustomed life for a period of a few months, more from exhaustion and disinterest in my own habits than as a result of any conscious attempt at self-improvement. I lived alone in a rela-tively modest apartment, with the singing tee shirt in a dresser drawer. When I practiced, I played variations on variations, as if the music and I had never met and were trying out new things on one another in the early stages of attraction. It was what the keys wanted, what the strings were asking for. I wondered how I would play on my next tour, and whether my fear of the rejection I expected from my fans was no more than a vanity.

Though I telephoned on holidays and sometimes on Sunday after-noons, I rarely thought of my home of origin and made no more than a handful of visits over the years to the abject town where my parents still lived. One day my mother called to tell me in a quavering voice that my father had died. As I packed for the funeral an impulse caused me to leave my suits in the closet, to dig through the dresser until I found the singing shirt and to pack it, muffling down its song. My return was front-page news in the weekly paper, and my appearance in informal dress was viewed as an expected eccentricity.

After the service, my father's spirit—or ghost, or soul, or whatever you like—approached me in the hallway outside the funeral home chapel. These things happen.

It was good of you to come, he said. The tone was typical of him.

You don't have to be sarcastic, I said.

My father's bald head shined, reminding me that his students had called him Chrome Dome. And, for some reason, that when I was a toddler he had called me Samson because my oversized hands made him dream he had spawned an athlete. His lifelong disappointment, apparently, had followed him into the afterlife.

Sarcastic? I'm dead serious. You could be in Tokyo or Berlin, tinkling the ivories for your accustomed fee. What is it these days? A hundred grand? Two hundred?

The shirt began to sing. Completely out of character, my father's spirit began to pop its neck to the rhythm. I couldn't believe it.

You don't like music!

This music I like.

I left my father be-bopping in the hall and made my way through the thinning crowd of mourners, climbed up to the small organ in the chapel. Of course the instrument was wrong, but I thought of Mozart's Rondo in A minor, then Schubert's Sonata in B-flat major. Then my hands began to play *My Funny Valentine*. The shirt went silent, listening.

The Apocalypse,
with Breath Mints

Jack and Annette are not hitting it off. Too bad because they are trapped in an SUV together for their entire annual trip between their fall/winter/spring home in West Monroe, LA, and their summer home in Grand Junction, CO, just the two of them and their springer spaniel, Bennie.

In some respects the situation is the same as usual. The not-hitting-it-off part in particular, and the Bennie. They have always had a Bennie, and Bennie has always been a springer spaniel. The realities of dog lives being what they are, the Bennies have been different Bennies, male and female, distinguished by qualifiers attached to the name. Fifteenth Street Bennie. Tragic Bennie, who died young, also known as Sweetest Bennie. Ball-nuts Bennie. Peanut Butter Bennie, and so on.

The Bennie line began in ancient history. During their grad student years, Jack and Annette lived in a big dilapidated house near campus. Members of the Banditos motorcycle gang lived in another part of the house. At that time, Jack made a living by cooking meth in the living room. The Banditos were the sales force for the product Jack created. This could lead to excitement. One night the sales persons engaged in a shootout with a rival gang in the street that ran in front of the house. Jack and Annette hid under their bed until the shooting stopped. Another night, after a party, they were involved in an episode of group sex, but they don't talk about that anymore.

In this same house, the Bennies got their beginning and their name. The origin of the name is disputed. According to Annette, the name derived quite naturally from the street term for Benzedrine, the brand name given to amphetamine sulfate, the first commercially available speed. According to Jack, Annette was known to complain about the smell of the meth lab, where Jack used benzene as a solvent. She also complained about the smell of the Banditos and of the springer spaniel puppy Jack had brought home, the primogenitor of Bennies, who was in fact the smelliest of all, Smelly Bennie. In Jack's version, he thought it would be funny to associate the puppy with things that irritated Annette, and thus the name.

Jack and Annette have a lot in common. They are both good at chemistry. They both like to eat and don't much care what. They were both more or less named for their parents. Jack's official name is John Jr., son of the late Big John. Annette's mother was Big Anne. Annette does not care for her mother's memory, but always says Jack worships Big John. Jack does not agree with the term worship.

Also, they have Time in common. One could speak of a lifetime, of course, but this is not a concept Time recognizes. Instead, Time recalls the feats and personhoods and the declines of Bennies, the impervious membranes of airborne argument launched above the morning paper, the wedding ring dissolved in nitric and hydrochloric acids, prepared in a molar mixture of precisely 1:3. Time sleeps with them and eats its portion of their food. It drips and gathers. At present it has gathered into a Lake of Time so vast they lose sight of the dock from which they once departed and have not yet glimpsed the opposite shore they know is fast approaching.

Also, some distance behind the present moment in their passage on the Lake of Time, they both retired. Annette was Director of Nursing at the largest hospital in West Monroe, LA. Jack worked at Dow Chemical, where he developed products that make it impossible for a bug to move or breathe. When Jack took that job right out of grad school it was almost the end of them, way back then.

This is how the waters of Time remember the moment:

Jack sits talking to the Dow recruiter in the florescent light of an intramural gym. Behind him, Annette walks a picket line together with most of the chemists they know. As Jack shakes hands with the recruiter and rises to leave, Annette puts her face, a young face, full and unlined, in his.

They make fucking napalm! she shouts at him. Little flecks of spittle land on his cheek.

It's work, Jack says, *people work.* He figures it is less risky than a meth lab. They do not speak to one another on the drive back to the dilapidated house.

As it turns out, Jack's career doesn't have anything to do with napalm. In fact, Jack becomes kind of a big deal in insecticide. He isn't crazy about Dow because they keep his patents, but he takes home a good living for a lot of years, plus bennies, which in this case do not refer to springer spaniels or amphetamine sulfate. Besides, he figures he has done some good. Asphyxiated a gazillion termites that would have chewed up people's houses, paralyzed a googolplex of mandibles about to chow down on somebody's corn.

When Jack makes this argument aloud, he can hear Annette's response before she says it:

Not to mention your many contributions to the field of birth defects.

Nobody ever proved that, Jack will answer.

To which Annette replies, *Then how come most of your inventions are banned in the U.S., even though they still sell them wherever they can, like in third-world countries where they get anything they want with bribes?*

They're only banned for home use, Jack says.

Annette gives him her face, no longer young, mocking incredulity.

This discussion has a longer lifespan than a tortoise. So do the ones about immigration, social welfare programs, foreign wars, and how Jack never wants to go anywhere or do anything and Annette needs friends and changes and he doesn't. How he doesn't listen and couldn't hear even if he did because he never wears his hearing aids.

He says she has never graduated from the counterculture. She says she would say he had lost his moral compass, if he ever had one in the first place. And they travel on.

Yet now, at this advanced position on their Lake of Time, nearing—in terms of the spatial dimension as represented by geography—Longview, TX, on the first leg of their twenty-first migration to the summerhouse, Jack perceives a difference that concerns him. Annette has no need to sense this difference because she is the difference. She shows no interest, Jack notices, in their venerable disagreements. She rarely raises up a favorite topic, and when Jack attempts a provocation she lets it fall through the air unanswered.

He is relieved when he hears her say, from her position in the passenger seat, *It's years past time to sell that house.* By this she means their primary domicile, the home in West Monroe, LA. The floor is now open for discussion. Jack adjusts the rearview to check on Bennie. Sometimes it upsets him when his parents argue. He is sleeping like an angel.

Jack considers his opportunity. Just wait a few laps of Time's waves and he will hear the following, he knows for certain:

The house is too much to take care of, is way too big for the two of them and a dog, always has been and now they live in barely any of it. And then: If they had kids and grandkids, who knows maybe great-grandkids by now, it would be different, but they don't. Think of all the resources that place eats up! The air conditioning punching holes in the atmosphere just to cool spaces they don't even use. The water they waste on the lawn. People should be thrown in jail for living like that. And all the property tax they pay—a kicker Annette knows comes closest to Jack's heart.

And Jack will take the floor and say the house is paid for, an asset that will keep appreciating as long as they hold onto it. Will say how much trouble it would be to move, especially at their age, and how much he hates moving. Will say he doesn't even want to think about it.

But what is this? Annette sits watching the lanes of freeways merge and lets all the potential of the house discussion trail away into a heavy silence. She listens to all the things that are not said, rewinds and plays them back, considers the vast dimensions of the Lake of Time and how long she has moved across it in this fashion, with this same person at the tiller, through these same fogs of words. Which makes her swell with anger.

Lost, Jack jumps ahead, hoping to spark the dialog.

The house is paid for, he ventures.

I need to pee, she says.

It's time to fill up anyway. They stop at a gas station with a convenience store attached. The station is crowded so Jack has to wait in line for a pump. Annette rises from the car without a word. Jack watches her back recede, all that mad puffing her bigger, like a pissed-off grizzly.

Jack is two cars back from the pump. He hears the guy at the pump invoking mother fuckers and sons of bitches. The guy slams the nozzle back in its seat and burns rubber off his tires as he pulls out. A woman puts in the hose and camps. She must have a tank like a reservoir. She shrugs at Jack like she's apologizing. He shrugs back. Years go by. Jack becomes aware that he also needs to pee. Needs it pretty bad. Finally the woman leaves and it's his turn.

But the pump runs super slow. Jack wonders if the station is running out of gas, but he hasn't heard about a shortage. He looks around at other pumps, but no one seems concerned. It takes a full minute to get a gallon in the tank. Bennie gazes out his open window at Jack, sympathetically. He notices the German shepherd in the back seat at the next pump over, and locks eyes with him. The shepherd is casually interested, wonders what Bennie smells like up close, what kind of food his people are packing, how much fun it would be to hump Bennie and demonstrate his dominance.

Jack gradually goes fugue, as he is inclined to do. Time ignores him. Seen from above, he is stationary at pump five of eight total, on a paved island in a paved world, a construct not unlike a termite mound, surrounded by exoskeletal creatures made of steel, fiberglass, and plastic, some stationary as he is, some rocketing in lines at deadly speed as if on missions of extreme importance to the mound.

How long can it take? Annette says, walking up, in the voice of Irritation itself, like the problem is him and not the pump. She's got a family-size bag of cheese puffs, already open.

I can't make it go any faster, Jack says.

Screw it. There are other stations.

By the time we get there it would take twice as long.

Always the expert, she says. She sits down in the car.

Jack's bladder sends distress signals. He wants a cheese puff. He keeps pumping.

On a previous migration, Annette read aloud from a magazine article entitled "The Four Signs That a Marriage Is in Trouble." The Sign Jack remembers is number 2: both partners are irritable a lot of the time. The other three Signs were pretty much on target too, as he recalls, but what did that really mean? You can't make rules for the way people behave like you can with chemical reactions. He glances at the pump.

How much have you put in? Annette's swollen voice through the window. Her swollen face, turned back toward him over the seat.

Twenty-six gallons, it looks like. Not possible, Jack thinks, but the pump is still moving, slow as ever.

The fucking tank only holds twenty-five! Annette says. *What are you doing, pouring gas on the ground?*

Jack looks down at his shoes and the puddle of gasoline he stands in. He reconstructs the engineering of the situation, which is this: Because the pump runs so slowly, the supposed cutoff valve fails to cutoff, thus the overfill, the overspill. Thus his puddle.

No, he says. *I think the pump is broken.*

Well, stop pumping and go get the money back!

Jack replaces the nozzle and pulls the car to the front of the store.

He goes inside, calculating again how much would remain after a fifty-fifty split of the 401k, the real estate, the not-so-secure Social Security, and again figures he could get by, so long as no catastrophe befalls him. Too bad catastrophe loves breathing on his neck, the older he gets. He sees himself in the summerhouse in Grand Junction, CO, but does not wish to imagine in detail an existence alone there, in deep, Valley-of-the-Shadow old age.

In the car, Annette thinks again how she will sell the house in West Monroe, LA, and move into the condo she has already picked out and decorated many times over, and what she will serve at the Free Annette party she will then throw for herself and her friends.

When Jack runs through his half of these thoughts he becomes a man too old to run, who nevertheless sprints through a forest in the dark, smack into two giant and familiar trees, one right after the other. Tree One: *Who gets the Bennie?* Tree Two: *Death.* Death is especially attracted to the thought of Jack on his own, Jack without Annette. Now Death joins Jack as he moves down the aisle between the bad coffee machine and the corn chips, Death, the Platonic ideal of serial killers, the mower-down of all the Bennies save one in the back seat, the murderer of Big John and Big Anne. This same Death mimics Jack in lockstep all the way to the door marked Men.

Jack goes to the urinal and afterwards the mirror. The face he sees is no longer the one he expects. Behind the face, Death leans against the wall.

Outside the door marked Men, God falls in step beside Death, beside Jack. Scientifically, Jack does not believe in God. God flickers as He/She/It walks. Jack picks up his own bag of cheese puffs. The three of them advance toward the clerk at the check-out counter.

You need to fix pump five, Jack tells the clerk. *It's barely moving.*

We don't own the pumps, the clerk says.

Can't you call somebody?

We call, but they never come. They don't care. People want a refund, I can't give it. We don't own the pumps.

Death puts a commiserating hand on Jack's shoulder. God checks out the chewing gum. Jack pays for the cheese puffs. They leave the store. God and Death pile in the back with Bennie. Annette doesn't notice.

Did you get a refund? she asks.

They don't own the pumps.

You stink like gas! You were just letting it run out on the ground, that whole time.

You think I wouldn't know if I were standing in gasoline?

God pats Bennie's head. Bennie wants a cheese puff.

I don't want to know what you know, Annette says. The swelling hasn't gone down. If anything, it has been nourished on cheese puffs and has grown.

Jack pulls out onto the highway. Silent, swollen miles pass. Bennie grows bored and falls asleep with his head in God's lap.

Jack, Jack, Jack, God says out of the blue, flickering, watching the cars pass in the opposite lanes. *What the heck? Is this it? Is this what you've done with your life? Killed off my fucking bugs? I like bugs!*

Jack finds this irritating. God is starting to remind him of Big John.

So what are You, anyway? Jack asks. *A He, a She, or an It?*

Fuck you, Jack! Annette says. *When was the last time you were Mr. Manley?*

I'm not talking to you, Jack says.

Really? Who the hell are you talking to?

Just call me They, God says.

You know what, Annette says, *when we get to Dallas you can drop me off at DFW. I'll get a flight up there and you and Bennie can drive.*

Why would we do that? Jack wants to know.

Because I don't want to be shut up in a car with you any more, He/She/It!

That sounds like the Apocalypse, Jack says. *I'm not ready for the Apocalypse.*

God does a weird thing with Their mouth, but doesn't say anything. Death appears to have fallen into a reverie. Annette stares out the window. Jack can only see the back of her neck, but it looks ready.

Everybody stays quiet. More miles pass, more. Dallas. Annette studies the towers on the horizon. The towers grow bigger.

At the airport, Jack unloads her bag. Bennie wakes up and watches as she opens her purse and fishes out some breath mints. She holds the tin out to Jack so he can take one. He takes two. He also takes this as a good sign.

After Annette disappears into a terminal, Death moves to the front and God stays in the rear, flickering like crazy. Jack looks back at Bennie. He's all smiles.

Acknowledgments

To Donna M. Johnson, my love and comrade in all things great and small, and our clan of children and grandchildren, who keep us proud and humble.

To my parents and my bookish relatives, who taught me to love words.

To Dana Curtis and her labor of love, Elixir Press, for bringing this book into the world.

To Ann Harleman, for selecting the book as the winner of the Elixir Fiction Award.

To Kyle McBride, designer extraordinaire, for the outstanding art on the front cover.

To all at the National Endowment for the Arts, for the fellowship that helped sustain me through a year.

To the Writers League of Texas, Writespace Houston, and The Loft in Minneapolis for opportunities to teach and learn from students.

To my own teachers, especially Jean Dugat, the beloved "Miss D."

To the poets and writers of my youth—especially the maestro of language Christopher Middleton—who let me pretend I was one of them.

To the Locos—Chaitali Sen, Rose Hansen Smith, Donna M. Johnson, Ed Latson—for close reads and supportive comment.

To the amazing Karen Russell, for her grand example, her luminosity of spirit and her unflagging generosity.

To Joy Williams, for boundless inspiration and the specific help with "The Apocalypse, with Breath Mints."

To Carolyn Kuebler, for her wise editorial counsel on "Banquo's Ghost."

To Naomi Shihab Nye, for making so many things possible on the poetry side of my existence.

To Keith and Rosmarie Waldrop, captains of legend at Burning Deck press, for their early vote of confidence.

And finally to all the editors, staff readers, and publishers who rejected versions of these stories and this book, for putting me back to work.

Stories included here were previously published in the following:

"Tapioca" – *Story*
"Banquo's Ghost" – *New England Review*
"The Goat's Eye" – *Meridian*, and subsequently in the anthology *This
    Side of the Divide: Stories from the American West*, from Baobab Press
"Smash and Grab" – *Valparaiso Fiction Review*
"The Comfort Zone" – published as "The Heart of Things" in *The
    Wordstock 10* anthology
"The Apocalypse, with Breath Mints" – *The Idaho Review*

About the Author

KIRK WILSON is the author of the poetry collection
SONGBOX (Trio House Press), winner of the 2020
Trio Award. Kirk's fiction, nonfiction, and poetry
are widely published in literary journals and antholo-
gies. His awards include an NEA Fellowship, Editor's
Awards and other prizes in all three genres, and two
Pushcart nominations. His past publications include a
poetry chapbook from Burning Deck press and a nonfiction crime book published in six editions in the US
and UK. He lives in Austin, Texas with his wife, the
memoirist Donna M. Johnson. Kirk's website is www.
KirkWilsonBooks.com.

ELIXIR PRESS TITLES

POETRY TITLES

Circassian Girl by Michelle Mitchell-Foust
Imago Mundi by Michelle Mitchell-Foust
Distance From Birth by Tracy Philpot
Original White Animals by Tracy Philpot
Flow Blue by Sarah Kennedy
A Witch's Dictionary by Sarah Kennedy
The Gold Thread by Sarah Kennedy
Rapture by Sarah Kennedy
Monster Zero by Jay Snodgrass
Drag by Duriel E. Harris
Running the Voodoo Down by Jim McGarrah
Assignation at Vanishing Point by Jane
    Satterfield
Her Familiars by Jane Satterfield
The Jewish Fake Book by Sima Rabinowitz
Recital by Samn Stockwell
Murder Ballads by Jake Adam York
Floating Girl (Angel of War) by Robert
    Randolph
Puritan Spectacle by Robert Strong
X-testaments by Karen Zealand
Keeping the Tigers Behind Us by Glenn J.
    Freeman
Bonneville by Jenny Mueller
State Park by Jenny Mueller
Cities of Flesh and the Dead by Diann Blakely
Green Ink Wings by Sherre Myers
Orange Reminds You Of Listening by Kristin
    Abraham
*In What I Have Done & What I Have Failed To
    Do* by Joseph P. Wood
Bray by Paul Gibbons
The Halo Rule by Teresa Leo
Perpetual Care by Katie Cappello
*The Raindrop's Gospel: The Trials of St. Jerome
    and St. Paula* by Maurya Simon
Prelude to Air from Water by Sandy Florian

Let Me Open You A Swan by Deborah Bogen
Cargo by Kristin Kelly
Spit by Esther Lee
Rag & Bone by Kathryn Nuerenberger
Kingdom of Throat-stuck Luck by George
    Kalamaras
Mormon Boy by Seth Brady Tucker
Nostalgia for the Criminal Past by Kathleen
    Winter
I will not kick my friends by Kathleen Winter
Little Oblivion by Susan Allspaw
Quelled Communiqués by Chloe Joan Lopez
Stupor by David Ray Vance
Curio by John A. Nieves
The Rub by Ariana-Sophia Kartsonis
Visiting Indira Gandhi's Palmist by Kirun Kapur
Freaked by Liz Robbins
Looming by Jennifer Franklin
Flammable Matter by Jacob Victorine
Prayer Book of the Anxious by Josephine Yu
flicker by Lisa Bickmore
Sure Extinction by John Estes
Selected Proverbs by Michael Cryer
Rise and Fall of the Lesser Sun Gods by Bruce
    Bond
Barnburner by Erin Hoover
Live from the Mood Board by Candice Reffe
Deed by Justin Wymer
Somewhere to Go by Laurin Becker Macios
*If We Had a Lemon We'd Throw It and Call
    That the Sun* by Christopher Citro
White Chick by Nancy Keating
The Drowning House by John Sibley Williams
Green Burial by Derek Graf
When Your Sky Runs into Mine by Rooja
    Mohassessy
Degrees of Romance by Peter Krumbach

FICTION TITLES

How Things Break by Kerala Goodkin
Juju by Judy Moffat
Grass by Sean Aden Lovelace
Hymn of Ash by George Looney
The Worst May Be Over by George Looney
Nine Ten Again by Phil Condon
Memory Sickness by Phong Nguyen
Troglodyte by Tracy DeBrincat

The Loss of All Lost Things by Amina Gautier
The Killer's Dog by Gary Fincke
Everyone Was There by Anthony Varallo
The Wolf Tone by Christy Stillwell
Tell Me, Signora by Ann Harleman
Far West by Ron Tanner
Out of Season by Kirk Wilson